More
Jonatha
and
# THE MURDER BOOK

"Kellerman really knows how to keep those pages turning."
—*The New York Times Book Review*

"The suspense heats up. . . . Kellerman creates vivid and compelling people."
—Cleveland *Plain Dealer*

"A page-turner . . . The pair uncover a sordid story of drugs, lustful and spoiled rich children, corruption and a cover-up that stretches high into the ranks of the powerful and wealthy."
—*The Toronto Sun*

"Often, mystery writers can either plot like devils or create believable characters. Kellerman stands out because he can do both. Masterfully."
—*USA Today*

"Kellerman has shaped the psychological mystery novel into an art form."
—*Los Angeles Times Book Review*

*Please turn the page*
*for more reviews. . . .*

"Kellerman tells his story with a mix of sharp dialogue, dead-on descriptions, and streamlined narrative that any writer might envy."
—*The Washington Post*

"If practice makes perfect, then Jonathan Kellerman has obviously had a lot of practice. His latest Alex Delaware novel is his best yet. . . . It is a page-turner that brings us to the end of Alex's evolution from psychiatrist to super sleuth. And if you think you have all the details worked out, there's a twist at the end to prove you can't out-think the author."
—*Witchita Falls Times Record News*

"No one does psychological suspense as well as Jonathan Kellerman."
—*Detroit Free Press*

"It's a pleasure to spend time with Kellerman's two sleuths."
—Baltimore *Sun*

"Kellerman does his usual masterful job of story-telling."
—*Abilene Reporter News*

"Kellerman's latest thriller illustrates the author's penchant for quick-wit dialogue. Segments with Delaware and Sturgis conversing are rapid-fire, each man exploring the other's hopes and fears while also advancing the case. Mutual analysis comes easy to the men, demon-wrestling is more difficult, and Kellerman explores that dichotomy nicely. . . . The journey from crime scenes to mind games is lucrative. . . . Kellerman has a way with advancing his two main players by exploring both their pasts and presents, forcing them to upchuck painful secrets, then leaving them ready for another day, slightly invigorated, as are his readers."
—*Book Street USA*

"Dramatic and satisfying . . . Kellerman does a masterful job of telling this tale of good and evil. . . . This is a page-turner that may make you back up and go for more."
—*Times Daily* (Florence, AL)

"A great plot, revealing much about Milo."
—*Toronto Globe & Mail*

## Books by Jonathan Kellerman

FICTION

*Alex Delaware Novels*
Bones (2008)
Compulsion (2008)
Obsession (2007)
Gone (2006)
Rage (2005)
Therapy (2004)
A Cold Heart (2003)
The Murder Book (2002)
Flesh and Blood (2001)
Dr. Death (2000)
Monster (1999)
Survival of the Fittest (1997)
The Clinic (1997)
The Web (1996)
Self-Defense (1995)
Bad Love (1994)
Devil's Waltz (1993)
Private Eyes (1992)
Time Bomb (1990)
Silent Partner (1989)
Over the Edge (1987)
Blood Test (1986)
When the Bough Breaks (1985)

*Other Novels*
Capital Crimes (With Faye Kellerman, 2006)
Twisted (2004)
Double Homicide (With Faye Kellerman, 2004)
The Conspiracy Club (2003)
Billy Straight (1998)
The Butcher's Theater (1988)

NONFICTION
With Strings Attached (2008)
Savage Spawn: Reflections on Violent Children (1999)
Helping the Fearful Child (1981)
Psychological Aspects of Childhood Cancer (1980)

FOR CHILDREN, WRITTEN AND ILLUSTRATED
Jonathan Kellerman's ABC of Weird Creatures (1995)
Daddy, Daddy, Can You Touch the Sky? (1994)

# THE MURDER BOOK

## AN ALEX DELAWARE NOVEL

# JONATHAN KELLERMAN

BALLANTINE BOOKS • NEW YORK

2008 Ballantine Books Mass Market Premium Edition

Copyright © 2002 by Jonathan Kellerman
Excerpt from *Bones* © 2008 by Jonathan Kellerman

Published in the United States by Ballantine Books, an imprint of The Random House Publishing Group, a division of Random House, Inc., New York.

BALLANTINE and colophon are registered trademarks of Random House, Inc.

Originally published in hardcover in the United States by Ballantine Books, an imprint of The Random House Publishing Group, a division of Random House, Inc., in 2002.

This book contains an excerpt from the forthcoming book *Bones* by Jonathan Kellerman. This excerpt has been set for this edition only and may not reflect the final content of the forthcoming edition.

ISBN 978-0-345-50854-6

Printed in the United States of America

www.ballantinebooks.com

OPM  9  8  7  6  5  4  3  2  1

To Faye

# CHAPTER
# 1

The day I got the murder book, I was still thinking about Paris. Red wine, bare trees, gray river, city of love. Everything that happened there. Now, this.

Robin and I flew in to Charles de Gaulle airport on a murky Monday in January. The trip had been my idea of a surprise. I'd pulled it together in one manic night, booking tickets on Air France and a room at a small hotel on the outskirts of the Eighth *arrondissement,* packing a suitcase for two, speeding the 125 freeway miles to San Diego. Showing up at Robin's room at the Del Coronado just before midnight with a dozen coral roses and a *voilà!* grin.

She came to the door wearing a white T-shirt and a hip-riding red sarong, auburn curls loose, chocolate eyes tired, no makeup. We embraced, then she pulled away and looked down at the suitcase. When I showed her the tickets, she turned her back and shielded me from her tears. Outside her window the night black ocean rolled, but this was no holiday on the beach. She'd left L.A. because I'd lied to her and put myself in danger. Listening to her cry now, I wondered if the damage was irreparable.

I asked what was wrong. As if I had nothing to do with it.

She said, "I'm just . . . surprised."

We ordered room-service sandwiches, she closed the drapes, we made love.

"Paris," she said, slipping into a hotel bathrobe. "I can't believe you did all this." She sat down, brushed her hair, then stood. Approached the bed, stood over me, touched me. She let the robe slither from her body, straddled me, shut her eyes, lowered a breast to my mouth. When she came the second time, she rolled away, went silent.

I played with her hair and, as she fell asleep, the corners of her mouth lifted. Mona Lisa smile. In a couple of days, we'd be queuing up as robotically as any other tourists, straining for a glimpse of the real thing.

She'd fled to San Diego because a high school chum lived there—a thrice-married oral surgeon named Debra Dyer, whose current love interest was a banker from Mexico City. ("So many white teeth, Alex!") Francisco had suggested a day of shlock-shopping in Tijuana followed by an indeterminate stay at a leased beach house in Cabo San Lucas. Robin, feeling like a fifth wheel, had begged off, and called me, asking if I'd join her.

She'd been nervous about it. Apologizing for abandoning me. I didn't see it that way, at all. Figured her for the injured party.

I'd gotten myself in a bad situation because of poor

planning. Blood had spilled and someone had died. Rationalizing the whole thing wasn't that tough: Innocent lives had been at stake, the good guys had won, I'd ended up on my feet. But as Robin roared away in her truck, I faced the truth:

My misadventures had little to do with noble intentions, lots to do with a personality flaw.

A long time ago, I'd chosen clinical psychology, the most sedentary of professions, telling myself that healing emotional wounds was how I wanted to spend the rest of my life. But it had been years since I'd conducted any long-term therapy. Not because, as I'd once let myself believe, I'd burned out on human misery. I had no problem with misery. My other life force-fed me *gobs* of misery.

The truth was cold: Once upon a time I *had* been drawn to the humanity and the challenge of the talking cure, but sitting in the office, dividing hour after hour by three quarters, ingesting other people's problems, had come to *bore* me.

In a sense, becoming a therapist had been a strange choice. I'd been a wild boy—poor sleeper, restless, overactive, high pain threshold, inclined to risk taking and injuries. I quieted down a bit when I discovered books but found the classroom a jail and raced through school in order to escape. After graduating high school at sixteen, I bought an old car with summer-job cash, ignored my mother's tears and my father's scowling vote of no confidence, and left the plains of Missouri. Ostensibly for college, but really for the threat and promise of California.

Molting like a snake. Needing something *new.*

Novelty had always been my drug. I craved insom-

nia and menace punctuated by long stretches of solitude, puzzles that hurt my head, infusions of bad
company and the delicious repellence of meeting up
with the slimy things that coiled under psychic rocks.
A racing heart jolted me happy. The kick start of
adrenaline punching my chest made me feel alive.

When life slowed down for too long, I grew hollow.

But for circumstance, I might've dealt with it by
jumping out of airplanes or scaling bare rocks. Or
worse.

Years ago, I'd met a homicide detective and that
changed everything.

Robin had put up with it for a long time. Now
she'd had enough and, sooner rather than later, I'd
have to make some kind of decision.

She loved me. I know she did.

Maybe that's why she made it easy for me.

# CHAPTER

# 2

In Paris, clichés are just fine.

You leave your hotel, step out into the winter drizzle, walk aimlessly until you find yourself at a café near the Jardin des Tuileries where you order overpriced baguettes and grainy, French-press coffee, then move on to the Louvre, where even during the off-season the lines prove daunting. So you cross the Seine on the Pont Royal, ignoring the motor din that washes the bridge, study the murk of the water below, try the Musée d'Orsay and murder your feet for a couple of hours, sucking in the fruits of genius. Then, deeper into the grubby side streets of the Left Bank, where you press yourself into the all-in-black throng, and laugh inwardly at an imagined wheezy accordion sound track overpowering the burping motor scooters and the whining Renaults.

It was early afternoon, near a shop in St. Germain, when it happened.

Robin and I had stepped into a dark, narrow men's haberdashery with a window full of aggressive neckties and slouching mannequins with pickpocket eyes. The rain had been coming in fitful bursts all day. The umbrella we'd cadged from the hotel concierge wasn't generous enough to shelter both of us and we each ended up more than half-wet. Robin didn't seem to mind. Her curls were beaded with droplets and her cheeks were flushed. She'd been quiet since we'd boarded the plane in L.A., sleeping for most of the flight, refusing dinner. This morning, we'd woken up late and barely talked. During the walk across the river, she seemed distracted—staring off at nothing in particular, holding my hand, then dropping it, then grabbing again and squeezing hard, as if scrambling to cover for some infraction. I put it down to jet lag.

The St. Germain stroll led us past a private school where beautiful, chittering adolescents spilled out onto the sidewalk, then a bookstore where I'd intended to browse until Robin pulled me into the clothing store, saying, "These are good silks, Alex. You could use something new."

The store peddled menswear, but smelled like a nail salon. The shopgirl was a skinny thing with hacked-up hair the color of eggplant rind and the anxiety of a new hire. Robin took a while thumbing through the goods, finally found me a very blue shirt and an extravagant red-and-gold tie of heavy weave, got my nod, asked the girl to wrap it up. Aubergine Tresses scurried to a back room and returned with a stout, cardiganed woman in her sixties who sized me up, took the shirt, and returned moments later brandishing a steaming iron in one hand and the garment in the other—newly pressed, on a hanger, shielded by a clear plastic bag.

"Talk about service," I said, as we returned to the street. "Hungry?"

"No, not yet."

"You didn't touch breakfast."

Shrug.

The stout woman had followed us out and was standing in the doorway of the shop. She looked up at the sky dubiously. Checked her watch. Seconds later, thunder clapped. Flashing us a satisfied smile, she went back inside.

The rain was harder, colder. I tried to draw Robin under the umbrella but she resisted, remained out in the open, raised her face and caught the spray full force. A man scrambling for cover turned to stare.

I reached for her again. She continued to balk, licked moisture from her lips. Smiled faintly, as if enjoying a private joke. For a moment I thought she'd share it. Instead, she pointed to a brasserie two doors up the street and ran in ahead of me.

"Bonnie Raitt," I repeated.

We were at a tiny table tucked in a corner of the clammy brasserie. The restaurant floor was a grubby mesh of white tile and the walls were cloudy mirrors and oft-painted brown woodwork. A clinically depressed waiter brought us our salads and wine as if service were harsh penance. Rain washed the front window and turned the city to gelatin.

"Bonnie," she said. "Jackson Browne, Bruce Hornsby, Shawn Colvin, maybe others."

"Three-month tour."

"At least three months," she said, still avoiding my eyes. "If it goes international, it could stretch longer."

"World hunger," I said. "Good cause."

"Famine and child welfare," she said.

"Nothing nobler."

She turned to me. Her eyes were dry and defiant.

"So," I said. "You're an equipment manager, now. No more guitar making?"

"There'll be luthiery involved. I'll be overseeing and repairing all the gear."

*I'll, not I'd. One-vote-election, nothing tentative.*

"When exactly did you get the offer?" I said.

"Two weeks ago."

"I see."

"I know I should've said something. It wasn't—it dropped in my lap. Remember when I was at Gold-Tone Studios and they needed those vintage archtops for that retro Elvis video? The tour manager happened to be in the next booth, watching some mixing, and ended up talking."

"Sociable fellow."

"Sociable woman," she said. "She had her dog with her—an English bulldog, a female. Spike started playing with her and we started talking."

"Animal magnetism," I said. "Is the tour dog-friendly, or do I keep Spike?"

"I'd like to take him along."

"I'm sure that'll thrill him to no end. When do you leave?"

"In a week."

"A week." My eyes hurt. "Lots of packing ahead."

She lifted her fork and pronged dead lettuce leaves. "I can call it off—"

"No," I said.

"I wouldn't have even considered it, Alex, not for the money—"

"Good money?"

She named the figure.

"Very good money," I said.

"Listen to what I'm saying, Alex: That doesn't matter. If you're going to hate me, it can be undone."

"I don't hate you, and you don't want it undone. Maybe you accepted the offer because I made you unhappy, but now that you've committed yourself, you're seeing all kinds of positives."

I craved argument but she didn't answer. The restaurant was filling, drenched Parisians seeking shelter from the downpour.

"Two weeks ago," I said, "I was running around with Milo on Lauren Teague's murder. Hiding what I was doing from you. I was stupid to think this trip would make a difference."

She pushed salad around. The room had grown hotter, smaller; scowling people crowded tiny tables, others stood huddled at the doorway. The waiter began to approach. Robin repelled him with a glare.

She said, "I've felt so alone. For a while. You were gone all the time. Putting yourself in *situations*. I didn't bring up the tour, because I knew you couldn't—shouldn't be distracted."

She rolled the side of a small fist along the table rim. "I guess I've always felt that what you do is important and that what I do is . . . just craft." I started to speak but she shook her head. "But this last time, Alex. Meeting with that woman, seducing her. Planning a damned *date* in order to—your intentions were good, but it still came down to seduction. Using yourself as a . . ."

"Whore?" I said. Thinking suddenly about Lauren

Teague. A girl I'd known a long time ago, from my quiet job. She'd sold her body, ended up head-shot and dumped in an alley . . .

"I was going to say 'lure.' Despite all we've had together—this supposed enlightened *relationship* we've got, you go about your own business. . . . Alex, basically you've built this whole other life from which I'm excluded. From which I *want* to be excluded."

She reached for her wineglass, sipped, made a face.

"Bad vintage?"

"Fine vintage. I'm sorry, baby, I guess it just comes down to timing. Getting the offer exactly when I was so down." She grabbed my hand, squeezed hard. "You love me, but you left me, Alex. It made me realize how alone I'd been for so long. We both were. The difference is, you enjoy going it alone—you get high on solitude and danger. So when Trish and I started talking and she told me she'd heard about my work—my reputation—and all of a sudden I realized I *had* a reputation, and here was someone offering me great money and the chance for something of my own, I said yes. Just blurted it out. And then driving home, I panicked, and said, *What did you just* do? And told myself I'd have to renege and wondered how I'd do it without looking like an idiot. But then I got home and the house was empty and all of a sudden I didn't *want* to renege. I went out to my studio and cried. I still might've changed my mind. I probably *would've*. But then you arranged that date with that tramp and . . . it felt completely right. It still does."

She looked out the rain-clouded window. "Such a beautiful city. I never want to see it again."

\* \* \*

The weather remained gray and wet and we kept to our room. Being together was agonizing: suppressed tears, edgy silences, too-polite chitchat, listening to the rain tormenting the dormer windows. When Robin suggested we return early to L.A., I told her I'd try to change her ticket but I'd be staying for a while. That hurt her but it also relieved her and the next day when the cab showed up to take her to the airport, I carried her bags, held her elbow as she got into the taxi, paid the driver in advance.

"How long will you be staying?" she said.

"Don't know." My teeth ached.

"Will you be back before I leave?"

"Sure."

"Please be, Alex."

"I will."

Then: the kiss, the smile, trembling hands concealed.

As the taxi drove away I strained for a look at the back of her head—a tremor, a slump, any sign of conflict, regret, grief.

Impossible to tell.

Everything moved too fast.

The break came on a Sunday—some young smiley-faced, ponytailed guy I wanted to punch, arriving with a large van and two paunchy roadies wearing black *Kill Famine Tour* T-shirts. Ponytail had a Milk-Bone for Spike, high fives for me. Spike ate out of his hand. How had the bastard known to bring the treat?

"Hi, I'm Sheridan," he said. "The tour coordinator." He wore a white shirt, blue jeans, brown boots, had a narrow body and a clean, smooth face full of optimism.

"Thought that was Trish."

"Trish is the overall tour manager. My boss." He glanced at the house. "Must be nice, living up here."

"Uh-huh."

"So you're a psychologist."

"Uh-huh."

"I was a psych major in college. Studied psycho-acoustics at UC Davis. Used to be a sound engineer." *How nice for you.* "Hmm."

"Robin's going to be part of something impor-tant."

"Hey," I said.

Robin came down the front stairs with Spike on a leash. She wore a pink T-shirt and faded jeans and tennis shoes and big hoop earrings, began directing the roadies as they loaded her valises and her toolboxes into the van. Spike looked stoned. Like most dogs, his emotional barometer is finely tuned and for the last few days he'd been uncommonly compliant. I went over and stooped to pat his knobby French bulldog head, then I kissed Robin, and recited, "Have fun," and turned my back and trudged up to the house.

She stood there, alongside Sheridan. Waved.

Standing at the door, I pretended not to notice, then decided to wave.

Sheridan got behind the wheel of the van and everyone piled in behind him.

They rumbled away.

Finally.

Now, for the hard part.

I started off determined to maintain my dignity. That lasted about an hour and for the next three days I turned off the phone, didn't check with my service or open the curtains or shave or collect the mail. I did read the paper because news coverage is heavily biased toward the hopeless. But other people's misfortunes failed to cheer me and the words danced by, as foreign as hieroglyphics. The little I ate, I didn't taste. I'm no problem drinker but Chivas became a friend. Dehydration took its toll; my hair got dry and my eyes creaked and my joints stiffened. The house, always too big, expanded to monstrous proportions. The air curdled.

On Wednesday, I went down to the pond and fed the koi because why should they suffer? That got me into a scut-work frenzy, scouring and dusting and sweeping and straightening. On Thursday I finally collected my messages. Robin had called every day, left numbers in Santa Barbara and Oakland. By Tuesday, she sounded anxious, by Wednesday, confused and annoyed and talking fast: The bus was headed for Portland. Everything was fine, Spike was fine, she was working hard, people were being great. *Iloveyouhopeyou'reokay.*

She called twice on Thursday, wondered out loud if I'd gone off on a trip of my own. Left a cell-phone number.

I punched buttons. Got: *Your call cannot be completed.*

Just after 1 P.M. I put on shorts and a workout shirt and sneakers, began stomping up Beverly Glen facing the traffic, easing into a clumsy jog when I felt loose enough, ending up running harder and faster and more punishingly than I'd done for years.

When I got home, my body burned and I could barely breathe. The mailbox down at the bridle path that leads up to the front gate was stuffed with paper and the postman had left several packages on the ground. I scooped it all up, dumped the batch on the dining room table, thought about more Scotch, drank a half gallon of water instead, returned to the mail and began sorting listlessly.

Bills, ads, solicitations from real estate brokers, a few worthy causes, lots of dubious ones. The packages were a psychology book I'd ordered a while back, a free sample of toothpaste guaranteed to heal my gums and feed my smile, and an eight-by-twelve rectangle wrapped in coarse blue paper with DR. A. DELAWARE and my address typed on a white label.

No return information. Downtown postmark, no stamps, just a meter. The blue paper, a heavy linen rag so substantial it felt like cloth, had been folded neatly and sealed tightly with clear tape. Slitting the folds revealed another snug layer of wrapping—pink butcher paper that I peeled away.

Inside was a three-ring binder. Blue, pebble-grain leather—substantial morocco, thumbed, grayed, and glossy in spots.

Stick-on gold letters were centered precisely on the front cover.

THE MURDER BOOK

I flipped the cover to a blank, black frontispiece. The next page was also black paper, encased in a stiff plastic jacket.

But not blank. Mounted with black, adhesive corner pockets was a photograph: sepia-toned, faded, with margins the color of too-whitened coffee.

Medium shot of a man's body lying on a metal table. Glass-doored cabinets in the background.

Both feet were severed at the ankles, placed just under ragged tibial stumps, like a puzzle in partial reassembly. No left arm on the corpse. The right was a mangled lump. Same for the torso above the nipples. The head was wrapped in cloth.

A typed caption on the bottom margin read: **East**

**L.A., nr. Alameda Blvd. Pushed under a train by common-law wife.**

The facing page featured a shot of similar vintage: Two sprawled gape-mouthed bodies—men—lying on a wooden plank floor, angled at forty degrees from each other. Dark stains spread beneath the corpses, tinted deep brown by age. Both victims wore baggy pants with generous cuffs, plaid shirts, lace-up work boots. Extravagant holes dotted the soles of the man on the left. A shot glass lay on its side near the elbow of the second, clear liquid pooling near the rim.

**Hollywood, Vermont Ave. Both shot by "friend" in dispute over money.**

I turned the page to a photo that appeared less antique—black-and-white images on glossy paper, close-up of a couple in a car. The woman's position concealed her face: stretched across the man's chest and sheathed by a mass of platinum blond curls. Polka-dot dress, short sleeves, soft arms. Her companion's head rested against the top of the car seat, stared up at the dome light. A black blood-stream trickled from his mouth, separated into rivulets when it reached his lapel, dribbled down his necktie. Skinny necktie, dark with a pattern of tumbling dice. That and the width of the lapel said the fifties.

**Silver Lake, near the reservoir, adulterers, he shot her, then put the gun in his mouth.**

Page 4: pale, naked flesh atop the rumpled covers of a Murphy bed. The thin mattress took up most of the floor space of a dim, wretched closet of a room. Undergarments lay crumpled at the foot. A young face stiffened by rigor, lividity pools at the shins, black-thatched crotch advertised by splayed legs, panty hose gathered to midcalf. I knew sexual positioning when I saw it so the caption was no surprise.

**Wilshire, Kenmore St., Rape-murder. Seventeen-year-old Mexican girl, strangled by boyfriend.**

Page 5: **Central, Pico near Grand, 89 y.o. lady crossing street, purse snatch turned to head-injury homicide.**

Page 6: **Southwest, Slauson Ave. Negro gambler beaten to death over craps game.**

The first color photo showed up on page ten: Red blood on sand-colored linoleum, the green-gray pallor that marked escape of the soul. A fat, middle-aged man sat slumped amid piles of cigarettes and candy, his sky blue shirt smeared purple. Propped near his left hand was a sawed-off baseball bat with a leather thong threaded through the handle.

**Wilshire, Washington Blvd. near La Brea, liquor store owner shot in holdup. Tried to fight back.**

I flipped faster.

**Venice, Ozone Avenue, woman artist attacked by neighbor's dog. Three years of arguments.**

**. . . Bank robbery, Jefferson and Figueroa. Teller resisted, shot six times.**

**. . . Strong-arm street robbery, Broadway and Fifth. One bullet to the head. Suspect stuck around, discovered still going through victim's pockets.**

**. . . Echo Park, woman stabbed by husband in kitchen. Bad soup.**

Page after page of the same cruel artistry and matter-of-fact prose.

Why had this been sent to me?

That brought to mind an old cartoon: *Why not?*

I thumbed through the rest of the album, not focusing on the images, just searching for some personal message.

Finding only the inert flesh of strangers.

Forty-three deaths, in all.

At the rear, a black end page with another centered legend, similar stick-on gold letters:

**THE END**

I hadn't talked to my best friend in a while, and that was fine with me.

After giving the D.A. my statement on Lauren Teague's murder, I'd had my fill of the criminal justice system, was happy to stay out of the loop until trial time. A wealthy defendant and a squadron of paid dissemblers meant that would be years away, not months. Milo had remained chained to the details, so I had a good excuse for keeping my distance: The guy was swamped, give him space.

The real reason was, I didn't feel like talking to him, or anyone. For years, I'd preached the benefits of self-expression but *my* tonic since childhood had been isolation. The pattern had been set early by all those bowel-churning nights huddled in the basement, hands over ears, humming "Yankee Doodle" in order to block out the paternal rage thundering from above.

When things got rough, I curled like a mollusk into a gray pocket of solitary confinement.

Now I had forty-three death shots on my dining room table. Death was Milo's raw material.

I called the West L.A. detectives' room.

\* \* \*

"Sturgis."

"Delaware."

"Alex. What's up?"

"I got something I thought you should see. Photo album full of what look like crime-scene photos."

"Photos or copies?"

"Photos."

"How many?"

"Forty-three."

"You actually counted," he said. "Forty-three from the same case?"

"Forty-three different cases. They look to be arranged chronologically."

"You 'got' them? How?"

"Courtesy the U.S. Postal Service, first class, downtown cancellation."

"No idea who might've favored you with this."

"I must have a secret admirer."

"Crime-scene shots," he said.

"Or someone takes very nasty vacations and decided to keep a scrapbook." The call-waiting signal clicked. Usually I ignore the intrusion, but maybe it was Robin from Portland. "Hold for a sec."

*Click.*

"*Hello,* sir," said a cheerful female voice. "Are you the person who pays the phone bill in the house?"

"No, I'm the sex toy," I said, and reconnected to Milo. Dial tone. Maybe he'd gotten an emergency call. I punched his desk number, got the West L.A. civilian receptionist, didn't bother to leave a message.

\* \* \*

The doorbell rang twenty minutes later. I hadn't changed out of my running clothes, hadn't made coffee or checked the fridge—the first place Milo heads. Looking at portraits of violent death would make most people lose their appetites, but he's been doing his job for a long time, takes comfort food to a whole new level.

I opened the door, and said, "That was quick."

"It was lunchtime, anyway." He walked past me to where the blue leather binder sat in full view, but made no move to pick it up, just stood there, thumbs hooked in his belt loops, big belly heaving from the run up to the terrace.

Green eyes shifted from the book to me. "You sick or something?"

I shook my head.

"So what's this, a new look?" A sausage finger aimed at my stubbled face.

"Maintaining a leisurely shaving schedule," I said.

He sniffed, took in the room. "No one chewing at my cuffs. El Poocho out back with Robin?"

"Nope."

"She's here, right?" he said. "Her truck's out front."

"You must be a detective," I said. "Unfortunately, false leads abound. She's out." I pointed to the book. "Check that out while I forage in the larder. If I can find anything that hasn't petrified, I'll fix you a sandwich—"

"No thanks."

"Something to drink?"

"Nothing." He didn't budge.

"What's the problem?" I said.

"How do I put this delicately," he said. "Okay: You look like shit, this place smells like an old-age home, Robin's truck is here but she isn't and my bringing her up makes your eyes drop to the floor like a suspect. What the hell's going on, Alex?"

"I look like shit?"

"To euphemize."

"Oh, well," I said. "Better cancel the photo shoot with *In Style*. And speaking of photography . . ." I held the book out to him.

"Changing the subject," he said, squinting down at me from his six-three vantage. "What do they call that in psychologist school?"

"Changing the subject."

He shook his head, kept his expression mild, folded his arms across his chest. But for spring-loaded tension around the eyes and mouth, he looked at peace. Pallid, acne-pitted face a bit leaner than usual, beer gut light-years from flat but definitely less bulge.

Dieting? On the wagon, yet again?

He'd dressed with uncommon color harmony: cheap but clean navy blazer, cotton khakis, white shirt with just a touch of fray at the neckline, navy tie, brand-new beige desert boots with pink rubber soles that squeaked as he shifted his weight and continued to study me. Brand-new haircut, too. The usual motif—clipped fuzzy at the sides and back, the top left long and shaggy, multiple cowlicks sprouting at the crown. A black forelock hooked over his pock-marked forehead. The hair from his temples to the bottoms of too-long sideburns had denatured to snow-white. The contrast with the black hair on top was unseemly—Mr. Skunk, he'd taken to calling himself.

"Spiffed and freshly barbered," I said. "Is this some new-leaf thing? Should I not attempt to feed you? Either way, take the damn book."

"Robin—"

"Later." I thrust the blue album at him.

He kept his arms folded. "Just put it back down on the table." Pulling out a pair of surgical gloves from the sets, he encased his hands in latex, studied the blue leather cover, opened the book, read the frontispiece, moved on to the first photo.

"Old," he murmured. "The tint and the clothes. Probably someone's creepy collection from the attic."

"Department shots?"

"Probably."

"A home collection pilfered from the evidence room?"

"Cases get filed away, someone gets itchy-fingered, who's gonna notice if one shot per file gets lifted."

"A cop?"

"A cop or a civilian ghoul. Lots of people have access, Alex. Some of them like the job because they dig blood."

" 'The murder book,' " I said. "Same title as an official case file."

"Same color, too. Whoever sent this knows procedure."

"Evoking procedure . . . why send it to me?"

He didn't answer.

I said, "It's not all antique. Keep going."

He studied several more photos, flipped back to the initial shot, then forward to where he'd left off. Resuming his inspection, picking up speed and skimming the horror, just as I had. Then he stopped. Stared at a photo toward the back of the book. Chunky knuckles swelled the gloves as he gripped the album.

"When exactly did you get this?"

"Today's mail."

He reached for the wrapping paper, took in the address, verified the postmark. Turned back to the album.

"What is it?" I said.

He placed the book on the table, open to the page that had stopped him. Resting his palms on either side of the album, he sat there. Ground his teeth. Laughed. The sound could have paralyzed prey.

Photograph Number 40.

A body in a ditch, muddy water pooled in the trough. Rusty blood on beige dirt. Off to the right side of the frame, dry weeds bristled. White-ink arrows were aimed at the subject, but the subject was obvious.

A young woman, maybe a teenager. Very thin—concave belly, rib cage washboard, fragile shoulders, spindly arms and legs. Slash and puncture wounds meshed her abdomen and neck. Curious black polka dots, too. Both breasts were gone, replaced by purplish discs the shape of marquis diamonds. Her angular face had been posed in profile, gazing to the right. Above her brow, where the hair should have been, floated a ruby cloud.

Purple ligature marks banded both wrists and ankles. More black dots speckled both legs—punctuation marks ringed with rosy halos—inflammation.

Cigarette burns.

Long white legs had been drawn up in a parody of sexual welcome.

I'd skimmed right past this one.

**Central, Beaudry Ave., body dump above 101 freeway on-ramp. Sex murder, scalped and strangled and slashed and burned. NS.**

" 'NS,' " I said. "No Solve?"

Milo said, "There was nothing else besides the book and wrapping? No note?"

"Nope. Just this."

He checked the blue wrapping again, did the same for the pink butcher paper, returned to the brutalized girl. Sat there for a long time until, finally, he freed one hand and rubbed his face as if washing without water. Old nervous habit. Sometimes it helps cue me in to his mood, sometimes I barely notice it.

He repeated the gesture. Squeezed the bridge of his nose. Rubbed yet again. Twisted his mouth and didn't relax it and stared some more.

"My, my," he said.

Several moments later: "Yeah, that would be my guess. No Solve."

" 'NS' wasn't appended to any of the other photos," I said.

No answer.

"Meaning this is what we're supposed to look at?" I said.

No answer.

"Who was she?" I said.

His lips slackened and he looked up at me and showed me some teeth. Not a smile, not even close to a smile. This was the expression a bear might take on when it spots a free meal.

He picked up the blue book. It vibrated. Shaking hands. I'd never seen that happen before. Emitting another terrible laugh, he repositioned the binder flat on the table. Squared the corners. Got up and walked into the living room. Facing the fireplace, he lifted a poker and tapped the granite hearth very softly.

I took a closer look at the mutilated girl.

His head shook violently. "What do you wanna fill your head with that for?"

"What about your head?" I said.

"Mine's already polluted."

*Mine, too.* "Who was she, Milo?"

He put the poker back. Paced the room.

"Who was she?" he said. "Someone turned into nothing."

# CHAPTER
# 5

The first seven killings weren't as bad as he'd thought.

Not bad at all, compared to what he'd seen in Vietnam.

The department had assigned him to Central Division, not far—geographically or culturally—from Rampart, where he'd paid a year of uniform dues, followed by eight months with Newton Bunco.

Managing to talk his way out of the initial Newton assignment: Vice. Wouldn't *that* have been a yuk-fest. Ha ha ha. The sound of one voice laughing.

He was twenty-seven years old, already fighting the battle of the bulge, brand-new to Homicide and not sure if he had the stomach for it. For any kind of police work. But, at this point—after Southeast Asia, what else was there?

A freshly minted Detective One, managing to hold on to his secret, though he knew there'd been talk.

No one confronting him directly, but he had ears.

*Something different about him—like he thinks he's better than anyone.*

*Drinks, but doesn't talk.*

*Doesn't shoot the shit.*

*Came to Hank Swangle's bachelor party but when they brought the groupie in and the gang bang started, where the fuck was he?*

*Free blow job and he splits.*

*Doesn't chase pussy, period.*

*Weird.*

His test scores and solve-rates and persistence got him to Central Homicide, where they paired him with a rail-thin forty-eight-year-old DII named Pierce Schwinn, who looked sixty and fancied himself a philosopher. Mostly, he and Schwinn worked nights, because Schwinn thrived in the dark: Bright lights gave the guy migraines, and he complained of chronic insomnia. No big mystery there, the guy popped decongestants like candy for a perpetually stuffed nose and downed a dozen cups of coffee per shift.

Schwinn loved driving around, spent very little time at his desk, which was a pleasant switch from the butt-numbing routine Milo had experienced at Bunco. But the downside was Schwinn had no attention span for white-collar work, couldn't wait to shove all the paperwork at his new junior partner.

Milo spent hours being a goddamned secretary, figured the best thing was to keep his mouth shut and listen, Schwinn had been around, must have something to offer. In the car, Schwinn alternated between taciturn and gabby. When he did talk, his tone got hyper and preachy—always making a *point*. Guy reminded him of one of his grad school professors at Indiana U. Herbert Milrad, inherited wealth, specialist on Byron. Lockjaw elocution, obese pear of a physique, violent mood swings. Milrad had figured

Milo out by the middle of the ...mester and tried to take advantage of it. Milo... far from clear about his sexuality, had declined ... tact. Also, he found Milrad physically repugnant.

Not a pretty scene, the Grand R...ection, and Milo knew Milrad would torment him ...e was finished with academia, any idea of a PhD. He finished the goddamned M.A. thesis by flogging the life out of poor Walt Whitman's words, escaped with a bare pass. Bored to tears, anyway, by the bullshit that passed for literary analysis, he left IU, lost his student deferment, answered a want ad at the campus student employment center, and took a job as a groundsman at the Muscatatuck National Wildlife Refuge, waiting for Selective Service to call. Five weeks later, the letter arrived.

By year's end, he was a medic wading through rice paddies, cradling young boys' heads and watching the departure of the barely formed souls, cupping steaming viscera in his hands—intestines were the big challenge, the way they slipped through his fingers like raw sausage. Blood browning and swirling as it hit the muddy water.

He made it home alive, found civilian life and his parents and brothers unbearable, struck out on a road trip, spent a while in San Francisco, learned a few things about his sexuality. Found SF claustrophobic and self-consciously hip, bought an old Fiat, and drove down the coast to L.A., where he stayed because the smog and the ugliness were reassuring. He knocked around for a while on temp jobs, before deciding police work might be interesting and why the hell not?

Then there he wa̲s̲ne unmarked in the parking
as he and Schwinn̲ ̲mple Street, eating green chile
lot of a Taco Tio̲ ̲ one of his quiet moods, eyes
burritos̲ ̲Schwir̲ ̲ ̲himself with no apparent plea-
jumpy s̲ ̲he ̲ ̲red̲
sure.

When the radio s̲n̲awked, Milo talked to the dis-
patcher, took down the details, said, "Guess we'd better shove off."

Schwinn said, "Let's eat first. No one's coming
back to life."

Homicide number eight.

The first seven had been no big deal, gross-out-
wise. Nothing whodunit about them, either. Like
nearly every Central case, the victims were all black
or Mexican and the same for the victimizers. When
he and Pierce showed, the only other white faces at
the scene would be uniforms and techs.

Black/brown cases meant tragedy that never hit
the papers, charges that mostly got filed and plea-
bargained, or, if the bad guy ended up with a really
stupid public defender, a long stay in county lockup,
then a quick trial and sentencing to the max allow-
able.

The first two calls had been your basic bar shootings, juicehead perpetrators drunk enough to stick
around when the uniforms arrived—literally holding
the smoking guns, putting up no resistance.

Milo watched Schwinn deal with fools, caught on
to what would turn out to be Schwinn's routine: First,
he'd mumbled an unintelligible Miranda to an un-
comprehending perp. Then he'd pressured the idiot
for a confession right there at the scene. Making sure

Milo had his pen and his pad out, was getting everything down.

"Good boy," he'd say afterward to the suspect, as if the asshole had passed a test. Over-the-shoulder aside to Milo: "How's your typing?"

Then back to the station, where Milo would pound the keys and Schwinn would disappear.

Cases Three, Four, and Five had been domestics. Dangerous for the responding blues, but laid out neatly for the D's. Three low-impulse husbands, two shootings, one stabbing. Talk to the family and the neighbors, find out where the bad guys were "hiding"—usually within walking distance—call for backup, pick 'em up, Schwinn mumbles Miranda. . . .

Killing Six was a two-man holdup at one of the discount jewelry outlets on Broadway—cheap silver chains and dirty diamond chips in cheesy ten-karat settings. The robbery had been premeditated, but the 187 was a fluke that went down when one of the stickup morons' guns went off by accident, the bullet zipping straight into the forehead of the store clerk's eighteen-year-old son. Big, handsome kid named Kyle Rodriguez, star football player at El Monte High, just happened to be visiting Dad, bringing the good news of an athletic scholarship to Arizona State.

Schwinn seemed bored with that one, too, but he did show his stuff. In a manner of speaking. Telling Milo to check out former employees, ten to one that's the way it would shake out. Dropping Milo off at the station and heading off for a doctor appointment, then calling in sick for the rest of the week. Milo did three days of legwork, assembled a list, zeroed in on a janitor who'd been fired from the jewelry store a month ago for suspected pilferage. Turned the guy up in an SRO hotel on Central, still rooming with the brother-in-law who'd been his partner in crime. Both bad guys were incarcerated and Pierce Schwinn showed up looking pink and healthy, and saying, "Yeah, there was no other possibility—did you finish the report?"

That one stuck in Milo's head for a while: Kyle Rodriguez's beefy bronze corpse slumped over the jewelry case. The image kept him up for more than a few nights. Nothing philosophical or theological, just general edginess. He'd seen plenty of young, healthy guys die a lot more painfully than Kyle, had long ago given up on making sense out of things.

He spent his insomnia driving around in the old Fiat. Up and down Sunset from Western to La Cienega, then back again. Finally veering south onto Santa Monica Boulevard.

As if that hadn't been his intention all along.

Playing a game with himself, like a dieter circling a piece of cake.

He'd never been much for willpower.

For three consecutive nights, he cruised Boystown. Showered and shaved and cologned, wearing a clean white T-shirt and military-pressed jeans and white tennies. Wishing he was cuter and thinner, but figuring he wasn't that bad if he squinted and kept his gut sucked in and kept his nerves under control by rubbing his face. The first night, a sheriff's patrol car nosed into the traffic at Fairfax and stayed two car lengths behind his Fiat, setting off paranoia alarms. He obeyed all the traffic rules, drove back to his crappy little apartment on Alexandria, drank beer until he felt ready to burst, watched bad TV, and made do with imagination. The second night, no sheriffs, but he just lacked the energy to bond and ended up driving all the way to the beach and back, nearly falling asleep at the wheel.

Night three, he found himself a stool in a bar near Larabee, sweating too damn much, knowing he was even tenser than he felt because his neck hurt like hell and his teeth throbbed like they were going to crumble. Finally, just before 4 A.M., before sunlight would be cruel to his complexion, he picked up a guy, a young black guy, around his own age. Well-dressed, well-spoken, education grad student at UCLA. Just about the same place as Milo, sexual-honesty-wise.

The two of them were jumpy and awkward in the guy's own crappy little grad student studio apartment on Selma south of Hollywood. The guy attending UCLA but living with junkies and hippies east of Vine because he couldn't afford the Westside. Polite chitchat, then . . . it was over in seconds. Both of them knowing there would be no repeat performance. The guy telling Milo his name was Steve Jackson but when he went into the bathroom, Milo spotted a date book embossed WES, found an address sticker inside the front cover. Wesley E. Smith, the Selma address.

Intimacy.

A sad case, Kyle Rodriguez, but he got over it by the time Case Seven rolled around.

A street slashing, good old Central Avenue, again. Knife fight, lots of blood all over the sidewalk, but only one db, a thirtyish Mexican guy in work clothes, with the homemade haircut and cheap shoes of a recently arrived illegal. Two dozen witnesses in a nearby *cantina* spoke no English and claimed blindness. This one wasn't even detective work. Solved courtesy of the blues—patrol car spotted a lurching perp ten blocks away, bleeding profusely from his own wounds. The uniforms cuffed him as he howled in agony, sat him down on the curb, called Schwinn and Milo, *then* phoned for the ambulance that transported the wretch to the jail ward at County Hospital.

By the time the detectives got there, the idiot was being loaded onto a gurney, had lost so much blood it was touch-and-go. He ended up surviving but gave up most of his colon and a bedside statement, pled guilty from a wheelchair, got sent back to the jail ward till someone figured out what to do with him.

Now, Number Eight. Schwinn just kept munching the burrito.

Finally, he wiped his mouth. "Beaudry, top of the freeway, huh? Wanna drive?" Getting out and heading for the passenger side before Milo could answer.

Milo said, "Either way," just to hear the sound of his own voice.

Even away from the wheel, Schwinn went through his jumpy predrive ritual. Ratcheting the seat back noisily, then returning it to where it had been. Checking the knot of his tie in the rearview, poking around at the corner of his lipless mouth. Making sure no cherry-colored residue of decongestant syrup remained.

Forty-eight years old but his hair was dead white and skimpy, thinning to skin at the crown. Five-ten and Milo figured him for no more than 140, most or it gristle. He had a lantern jaw, that stingy little paper cut of a mouth, deep seams scoring his rawboned face, and heavy bags under intelligent, suspicious eyes. The package shouted dust bowl. Schwinn had been born in Tulsa, labeled himself Ultra-Okie to Milo minutes after they'd met.

Then he'd paused and looked the young detective in the eye. Expecting Milo to say something about his own heritage.

*How about Black Irish Indiana Fag?*

Milo said, "Like the Steinbeck book."

"Yeah," said Schwinn, disappointed. "*Grapes of Wrath*. Ever read it?"

"Sure."

"I didn't." Defiant tone. "Why the fuck should I? Everything in there I already learned from my daddy's stories." Schwinn's mouth formed a poor excuse for a smile. "I hate books. Hate TV and stupid-ass radio, too." Pausing, as if laying down a gauntlet.

Milo kept quiet.

Schwinn frowned. "Hate sports, too—what's the point of all that?"

"Yeah, it can get excessive."

"You've got the size. Play sports in college?"

"High school football," said Milo.

"Not good enough for college?"

"Not nearly."

"You read much?"

"A bit," said Milo. Why did that sound confessional?

"Me too." Schwinn put his palms together. Aimed

those accusatory eyes at Milo. Leaving Milo no choice.

"You hate books but you read."

"Magazines," said Schwinn, triumphantly. "Magazines cut to the chase—take your *Reader's Digest*, collects all the bullshit and condenses it to where you don't need a shave by the time you finish. The other one I like is *Smithsonian*."

Now there was a surprise.

"*Smithsonian*," said Milo.

"Never heard of it?" said Schwinn, as if relishing a secret. "The museum, in Washington, they put out a magazine. My wife went and subscribed to it and I was ready to kick her butt—just what we needed, more paper cluttering up the house. But it's not half-bad. They've got all sorts of stuff in there. I feel educated when I close the covers, know what I mean?"

"Sure."

"Now *you*," said Schwinn, "they tell me you *are* educated." Making it sound like a criminal charge. "Got yourself a master's degree, is that right?"

Milo nodded.

"From where?"

"Indiana U. But school isn't necessarily education."

"Yeah, but sometimes it is—what'd you study at Indiana *Yooo*?"

"English."

Schwinn laughed. "God loves me, sent me a partner who can spell. Anyway, give me magazines and burn all the books as far as I'm concerned. I like science. Sometimes when I'm at the morgue I look at medical books—forensic medicine, abnormal psychology, even anthropology 'cause they're learning to do stuff with bones." His own bony finger wagged. "Let me tell you something, boy-o: One day, science is gonna be a big damn deal in our business. One day, to be doing our job a guy's gonna have to be a scientist—show up at a crime scene, scrape the db, carry a little microscope, learn the biochemical makeup of every damn scrote the vic hung out with for the last ten years."

"Transfer evidence?" Milo said. "You think it'll get that good?"

"Sure, yeah," Schwinn said, impatiently. "Right now transfer evidence is for the most part useless bullshit, but wait and see."

They had been driving around Central on their first day as partners. Aimlessly, Milo thought. He kept waiting for Schwinn to point out known felons, hot spots, whatever, but the guy seemed unaware of his surroundings, all he wanted to do was talk. Later, Milo would learn that Schwinn had plenty to offer. Solid detective logic and basic advice. ("Carry your own camera, gloves, and fingerprint powder. Take care of your own self, don't depend on anyone.") But right now, this first day, riding around—everything— seemed pointless.

"Transfer," said Schwinn. "All we can transfer now is ABO blood type. What a crock. Big deal, a million scrotes are type O, most of the rest are A, so what does *that* do? That and hair, sometimes they take hair, put it in little plastic envelopes, but what the fuck can they do with it, you always get some Hebe lawyer proving hair don't mean shit. No, I'm talking serious science, something nuclear, like the way they date fossils. Carbon dating. One day, we'll be anthropologists. Too bad you don't have a master's degree in anthropology . . . can you type okay?"

A few miles later, Milo was taking in the neighborhood on his own, studying faces, places, when Schwinn proclaimed: "English won't do you a damn bit of good, boy-o, 'cause our customers don't talkie mucho *English*. Not the Mexes, not the niggers, either—not unless you want to call that jive they give you English."

Milo kept his mouth shut.

"Screw English," said Schwinn. "*Fuck* English in the ass with a hydrochloric acid dildo. The wave of the future is science."

They hadn't been told much about the Beaudry call. Female Caucasian db, discovered by a trash-picker sifting through the brush that crested the freeway on-ramp.

Rain had fallen the previous night and the dirt upon which the corpse had been placed was poor-drainage clay that retained an inch of grimy water in the ruts.

Despite a nice soft muddy area, no tire tracks, no footprints. The ragpicker was an old black guy named Elmer Jacquette, tall, emaciated, stooped, with Parkinsonian tremors in his hands that fit with his agitation as he retold the story to anyone who'd listen.

"And there it was, right out there, Lord Jesus . . ."

No one was listening anymore. Uniforms and crime-scene personnel and the coroner's man were busy doing their jobs. Lots of other people stood around, making small talk. Flashing vehicles blocked Beaudry all the way back to Temple as a bored-looking patrolman detoured would-be freeway speeders.

Not too many cars out: 9 P.M. Well past rush hour. Rigor had come and gone, as had the beginnings of putrefaction. The coroner was guesstimating a half day to a day since death, but no way to know how long the body had been lying there or what temperature it had been stored at. The logical guess was that the killer had driven up last night, after dark, placed the corpse, zipped right onto the 101, and sped off happy.

No passing motorist had seen it, because when you were in a hurry, why would you study the dirt above the on-ramp? You never get to know a city unless you walk. Which is why so few people know L.A., thought Milo. After living here for two years, he still felt like a stranger.

Elmer Jacquette walked all the time, because he had no car. Covered the area from his East Hollywood flop to the western borders of downtown, poking around for cans, bottles, discards he tried to peddle to thrift shops in return for soup kitchen vouchers. One time, he'd found a working watch—gold, he thought, turned out to be plated but he got ten bucks for it, anyway, at a pawnshop on South Vermont.

*He'd* seen the body right away—how could you not from up close, all pale in the moonlight, the sour smell, the way the poor girl's legs had been bent and spread—and his gorge had risen immediately and soon his franks-and-beans dinner was coming back the wrong way.

Jacquette had the good sense to run a good fifteen feet from the body before vomiting. When the uniforms arrived, he pointed out the emetic mound, apologizing. Not wanting to annoy anyone. He was sixty-eight years old, hadn't served state time since fifteen years ago, wasn't going to annoy the police, no way.

*Yessir, nossir.*

They'd kept him around, waiting for the detectives to arrive. Now, the men in suits were finally here and Jacquette stood over by one of the police cars as someone pointed him out and they approached him, stepping into the glare of those harsh lights the cops had put all over the place.

Two suits. A skinny white-haired redneck type in an old-fashioned gray sharkskin suit and a dark-haired, pasty-faced heavyset kid whose green jacket and brown pants and ugly red-brown tie made Elmer wonder if nowadays *cops* were shopping at thrift shops.

They stopped at the body first. The old one took one look, wrinkled his nose, got an annoyed look on his face. Like he'd been interrupted in the middle of doing something important.

The fat kid was something else. Barely glanced at the body before whipping his head away. Bad skin, that one, and he'd gone white as a sheet, started rubbing his face with one hand, over and over.

Tightening up that big heavy body of his like *he* was ready to lose his lunch.

Elmer wondered how long the kid had been on the job, if he'd actually blow chunks. If the kid did heave, would he be smart enough to avoid the body, like Elmer had?

'Cause this kid didn't look like no veteran.

# CHAPTER
# 6

This was worse than Asia.

No matter how brutal it got, war was impersonal, human chess pieces moving around the board, you fired at shadows, strafed huts you pretended were empty, lived every day hoping you wouldn't be the pawn that flipped. Reduce someone to The Enemy, and you could blow off his legs or slice open his belly or napalm his kids without knowing his name. As bad as war got, there was always the chance for making nice sometime in the future—look at Germany and the rest of Europe. To his father, an Omaha Beach alumnus, buddying up to the krauts was an abomination. Dad curled his lip every time he saw a "hippie-faggot in one of those Hitler beetle-cars." But Milo knew enough history to understand that peace was as inevitable as war and that as unlikely as it seemed, one day Americans might be vacationing in Hanoi.

War wounds had a chance of healing *because* they weren't personal. Not that the memory of guts slipping through his hands would fade, but maybe, somewhere off in the future . . .

But *this*. This was nothing *but* personal. Reduction of human form to meat and juice and refuse. Creating the antiperson.

He took a deep breath and buttoned his jacket and managed another look at the corpse. How old could she be, seventeen, eighteen? The hands, about the only parts of her not bloody, were smooth, pale, free of blemish. Long, tapering fingers, pink-polished nails. From what he could tell—and it was hard to tell anything because of the damage—she'd had delicate features, might've been pretty.

No blood on the hands. No defense wounds . . .

The girl was frozen in time, a heap of ruin. Aborted—like a shiny little wristwatch, stomped on, the crystal shattered.

Manipulated after death, too. The killer spreading her legs, tenting them, pointing the feet at a slight outward angle.

Leaving her out in the open—horrible statuary.

*Overkill*, the assistant coroner had pronounced, as if you needed a medical degree for *that*.

Schwinn had told Milo to count wounds, but the task wasn't that simple. The slashes and cuts were straightforward, but did he count the ligature burns around both wrists and ankles as wounds? And what about the deep, angry red trench around her neck? Schwinn had gone off to get his Instamatic—always a shutterbug—and Milo didn't want to ask him— loathed coming across uncertain, the rookie he was.

He decided to include the ligatures in a separate column, continued making hash marks. Reviewed his count of the knife wounds. Both premortem and after death, the coroner was guessing. One, two, three, four . . . he confirmed fifty-six, began his tally of the cigarette burns.

Inflammation around the singed circles said the burns had been inflicted before death.

Very little spent blood at the scene. She'd been killed somewhere else, left here.

But lots of dried blood atop the head, forming a blackening cap that kept attracting the flies.

The finishing touch: scalping her. Should that be counted as one giant wound, or did he need to peer under the blood, see how many times the killer had hacked away the skin?

A cloud of night gnats circled above the body, and Milo scatted it away, noted "removal of cranial skin," as a separate item. Drawing the body and topping it with the cap, his lousy rendering making the blood look like a beanie, so inadequately offensive. He frowned, closed his pad, stepped back. Studied the body from a new perspective. Fought back yet another wave of nausea.

The old black guy who'd found her had heaved his cookies. From the moment Milo had seen the girl, he'd struggled not to do the same. Tightening his bowels and his gut, trying to come up with a mantra that would do the trick.

*You're no virgin, you've seen worse.*

Thinking of the worst: *melon-sized holes in chests, hearts bursting—that kid, that Indian kid from New Mexico—Bradley Two Wolves—who'd stepped on a mine and lost everything below the navel but was still talking as Milo pretended to do something for him. Looking up at Milo with soft brown eyes—alive eyes, dear God—talking calmly, having a goddamn conver-*

sation with nothing left and everything leaki..
That *was* worse, right? Having to talk back to the
upper half of Bradley Two Wolves, chitchatting about
Bradley's pretty little girlfriend in Galisteo, Bradley's
dreams—once he got back to the States, he was
gonna marry Tina, get a job with Tina's dad putting
up adobe fences, have a bunch of kids. Kids. With
nothing below the—Milo smiled down at Bradley
and Bradley smiled back and died.

That had been worse. And back then Milo had
managed to keep his cool, keep the conversation
going. Cleaning up afterward, loading half-of-
Bradley in a body bag that was much too roomy.
Writing out Bradley's death tag for the flight surgeon
to sign. For the next few weeks, Milo had smoked a
lot of dope, sniffed some heroin, done an R and R in
Bangkok, where he tried some opium. He'd even hazarded an attempt at a skinny Bangkok whore. That
hadn't gone so great, but bottom line: He'd *maintained*.

*You can handle this, stupid.*

*Breathe slowly, don't give Schwinn something else
to lecture about—*

Schwinn was back now, clicking away with his Instamatic. The LAPD photographer had spotted the
little black plastic box, caressed his Nikon, smirked.
Schwinn was oblivious to the contempt, in his own
little world, crouching on all sides of the body. Getting close to the body, closer than Milo had hazarded,
not even bothering to shoo the gnats swarming his
white hair.

"So what do you think, boy-o?"

"About . . . ?" said Milo.

*Click click click.* "The bad guy—what's your gut telling you about him?"

"Maniac."

"Think so?" Schwinn said, almost absently. "Howling-lunatic-drooling-crazyman?" He moved away from Milo, kneeled right next to the flayed skull. Close enough to kiss the mangled flesh. Smiled. "Look at this—just bone and a few blood vessels, sliced at the back . . . a few tears, some serrations . . . real sharp blade." *Click click.* "A maniac . . . some shout-at-the-moon Apache warrior? *You,* naughty squaw, *me* scalpum?"

Milo battled another abdominal heave.

Schwinn got to his feet, dangled the camera from its little black string, fiddled with his tie. His Okie hatchet face bore a satisfied look. Cool as ice. How often had *he* seen this? How often did this kind of thing come up in Homicide? The first seven—even Kyle Rodriguez, had been tolerable compared to this. . . .

Schwinn pointed at the girl's propped-up legs. "See the way he posed her? He's talking to us, boy-o. Talking through her, putting words in her mouth. What's he want her to say, boy-o?"

Milo shook his head.

Schwinn sighed. "He wants her to say, 'Fuck me.' To the whole world—'C'mon over, whole damn world, and fuck me silly, anyone wants to do anything to me, they can 'cause I got no power.' He's using her like . . . a puppet—you know how kids move puppets around, get puppets to say things they're too scared to say for themselves? This guy's like that, only he likes big puppets."

"He's scared?" said Milo doubtfully.

"What the fuck do *you* think?" said Schwinn. "We're talking about a coward, can't talk to women, get laid in any normal way. Which isn't to say he's a wimpy type. He could be macho. He's sure nervy enough, taking the time for that." Backward glance at the legs. "Posing her right out in the open, risking being seen. I mean, think about it: You had your fun with the body, needed to get rid of the body, you're carrying it around in your car, want to dump it, where would you go?"

"Somewhere remote."

"Yeah, 'cause you're not a nervy killer, to you it would just be dumping. Not our boy. On the one hand, he's smart. Doing it right by the freeway, once he's finished, he can get back on, no one's conspicuous on the 101. He does it after dark, checks to make sure no one's watching, pulls over, arranges her, then zoom zoom zoom. It's a decent plan. It could work nice, especially this late, rush hour's over. But taking the time to *stop* is still a risk, just to play puppet. So this wasn't about dumping. This was showing off—having his cake and eating it twice. He ain't stupid or crazy."

"Playing a game," said Milo, because that sounded agreeable. Thinking about chess, but unable to really reconcile this with any game.

"'*Look at me,*'" said Schwinn. "That's what he's telling us. 'Look what I can do.' It's not enough he overpowered her and fucked the hell out of her—hundred to one we'll find a mess of semen up her twat, her ass. What he wants now is to share her with the world. I control her, everyone hop on board."

"Gang bang," said Milo, hoarsely, flashing back to Hank Swangle's party at Newton Division. The Newton groupie, a heavy, blond bank clerk, prim and upright during the day, a whole other life when it came to cops. Pillowy, drunk, and glazed when collegial hands had shoved Milo into the room with her. The groupie reaching out to Milo, lipstick smeared, mouthing, "Next." Like a take-a-number line in a bakery. He'd muttered some excuse, hurried out . . . why the hell was he thinking of that, now? And now the nausea was returning—his hands throbbed, he was clenching them.

Schwinn was staring at him.

He forced himself to release the fingers, kept his voice level. "So he's more rational than a maniac. But we are talking someone mentally abnormal, right? Someone normal wouldn't do this." Hearing the stupidity of each word as it tumbled out.

Schwinn smiled again. "Normal. Whatever the hell that means." He turned his back on Milo, walked away without a word, swinging his camera. Stood off by himself next to the coroner's van, leaving Milo with his bad sketches and compulsive hash marks.

*Whatever the hell that means.*

A knowing smile. Loose talk about Milo's sexuality wafting from Rampart and Newton to Central? Was that why the guy was so hostile?

Milo's hands were clenching again. He'd started to think of himself as maybe fitting in, handling the first seven 187s okay, getting into the 187 groove and thinking he might stick with Homicide, murder would turn out to be something he could finally live with.

Now he cursed the world, got close to the girl. Closer even than Schwinn. Taking in the sights, the smell, every wound—drinking in the horror, telling himself *shut up, idiot, who the hell are you to complain, look at her.*

But the rage intensified, flowed over him, and suddenly he felt hard, cruel, vengeful, analytic.

Seized by a rush of *appetite*.

Trying to make sense of this. Needing to.

He smelled the girl's rot. Wanted, suddenly, to enter her hell.

It was nearly eleven by the time he and Schwinn were back in the unmarked.

"You drive again," said Schwinn. No sign of any hostility, no more possible double entendres, and Milo started to think he'd been paranoid about the normalcy comment. Just Schwinn flapping his lips, because the guy was like that.

He started up the engine. "Where to?"

"Anywhere. Tell you what, take the freeway for a couple exits, then turn around, go back downtown. I need to think."

Milo complied. Cruising down the ramp, as the killer had done. Schwinn stretched and yawned, sniffed and produced his bottle of decongestant and took a long red swallow. Then he leaned over and switched off the radio, closed his eyes, fooled with the corners of his lips. This was going to be one of those silent stretches.

It lasted until Milo was back on city streets, driving up Temple, passing the Music Center and the dirt lots that surrounded it. Lots of empty space as the rich folk planned additional shrines to culture. Talking urban renewal—pretending anyone would ever bother with this poor excuse for a downtown, pretending it wasn't a cement grid of government buildings where bureaucrats worked the day shift and couldn't wait to get the hell out of there and everything got cold and black at night.

"So what's next?" said Schwinn. "On the girl. What do you think?"

"Find out who she was?"

"Shouldn't be too hard, those smooth nails, nice straight teeth. If she was a street slut, her comedown was recent. Someone'll miss her."

"Should we start with Missing Persons?" said Milo.

"*You'll* start with Missing Persons. Start calling tomorrow morning 'cause MP doesn't staff heavy at night, good luck trying to get those guys off their asses at this hour."

"But if she was reported missing, getting the info tonight would give us a head start—"

"On what? This is no race, boy-o. If our bad boy's out of town, he's long gone, anyway. If not, a few hours won't make a damn bit of difference."

"Still, her parents have got to be worried—"

"Fine, amigo," said Schwinn. "Be a social worker. I'm going home."

No anger, just that know-it-all smugness.

"Want me to head back to the station?" said Milo.

"Yeah, yeah. No, forget that. Pull over—*now,* boy-o. Over *there,* yeah yeah yeah stop next to that *bus* bench."

The bench was a few yards up, on the north side of

Temple. Milo was in the left-hand lane and had to turn sharply not to overshoot. He edged to the curb, looked around to see what had changed Schwinn's mind.

Dark, empty block, no one around—no, there *was* someone. A figure emerging from the shadows. Walking west. Walking quickly.

"A source?" said Milo, as the shape took form. Female form.

Schwinn tightened his tie knot. "Stay put and keep the engine going." He got out of the car, quickly, got to the sidewalk just in time to meet the woman. Her arrival was heralded by spike heels snapping on the pavement.

A tall woman—black, Milo saw, as she shifted into the streetlight. Tall and busty. Maybe forty. Wearing a blue leather mini and a baby blue halter top. Jumbo pile of henna-colored waves atop her head, what looked to be ten pounds of hair.

Schwinn, standing facing her, looking even skinnier than usual. Legs slightly spread. Smiling.

The woman smiled back. Offered both cheeks to Schwinn. One of those Italian movie greetings.

A few moments of conversation, too low for Milo to make out, then both of them got in the backseat of the unmarked.

"This is Tonya," said Schwinn. "She's a good pal of the department. Tonya, meet my brand-new partner, Milo. He's got a master's degree."

"Ooh," said Tonya. "Are you masterful, honey?"

"Nice to meet you, ma'am."

Tonya laughed.

"Start driving," said Schwinn.

"Master's degree," said Tonya, as they pulled away.

At Fifth Street, Schwinn said, "Turn left. Drive into the alley behind those buildings."

"Masturbator's degree?" said Tonya.

"Speaking of which," said Schwinn. "My darling dear."

"Ooh, I love when you talk that way, Mr. S."

Milo reduced his speed.

Schwinn said, "Don't do that, just drive regular—turn again and make a right—go east. Alameda, where the factories are."

"Industrial revolution," said Tonya, and Milo heard something else: the rustle of clothing, the *sprick* of a zipper undone. He hazarded one look in the rearview, saw Schwinn's head, resting against the back of the seat. Eyes closed. Peaceful smile. Ten pounds of henna bobbing.

A moment later: "Oh, yes, Miss T. I missed you, did you know that?"

"Did you, baby? Aw, you're just saying that."

"Oh, no, it's true."

"*Is* it, baby?"

"You bet. Miss me, too?"

"You know I do, Mr. S."

"Every day, Miss T?"

"Every day, Mr. S.—c'mon, baby, move a little, help me with this."

"Happy to help," said Schwinn. "Protect and serve."

Milo forced his eyes straight ahead.

No sound in the car but heavy breathing.

"Yeah, yeah," Schwinn was saying now. His voice weak. Milo thought: This is what it takes to knock off the asshole's smugness.

"Oh yeah, just like that, my darling . . . dear. Oh, yes, you're . . . a . . . specialist. A . . . scientist, yes, yes."

# CHAPTER

# 7

Schwinn told Milo to drop Tonya off on Eighth near Witmer, down the block from the Ranch Depot Steak House.

"Get yourself a hunk of beef, darling." Slipping her some bills. "Get yourself a lovely T-bone with one of those giant baked potatoes."

"Mr. S.," came the protest. "I can't go in there dressed like this, they won't serve me."

"With this they will." Another handful of paper pressed into her hand. "You show this to Calvin up front, tell him I sent you—you have any problem, you let me know."

"You're sure?"

"You know I am."

The rear door opened, and Tonya got out. The smell of sex hung in the car. Now the night filtered in, cool, fossil-fuel bitter.

"Thank you, Mr. S." She extended her hand. Schwinn held on to it.

"One more thing, darling. Hear of any rough johns working the Temple-Beaudry area?"

"How rough?"

"Ropes, knives, cigarette burns."

"Ooh," said the hooker, with pain in her voice. "No, Mr. S, there's always lowlife, but I heard nothing like that."

Pecks on cheeks. Tonya clicked her way toward the restaurant, and Schwinn got back in front. "Back to the station, boy-o."

Closing his eyes. Self-satisfied. At Olive Street, he said: "That's a very intelligent nigger, boy-o. Given the opportunity a free, white woman woulda had, she woulda made something of herself. What's that about?"

"What do you mean?"

"The way we treat niggers. Make sense to you?"

"No," said Milo. Thinking: What the hell is this *lunatic* about?

Then: Why hadn't Schwinn offered the hooker to *him*?

Because Schwinn and Tonya had something special? Or because he *knew*?

"What it says," offered Schwinn. "The way we treat niggers, is that sometimes smart doesn't count."

Milo dropped him off at the Central Division parking lot, watched him get into his Ford Fairlane and drive off to Simi Valley, to the wife who liked books.

Alone, at last.

For the first time since the Beaudry call, he was breathing normally.

He entered the station, climbed the stairs, hurried to the scarred metal desk they'd shoved into a corner of the Homicide room for him. The next three hours were spent phoning Missing Persons bureaus at every station and when that didn't pay off, he extended the search to various sheriff's substations and departments of neighboring cities. Every office kept its own files, no one coordinated, each folder had to be pulled by hand, and MP skeleton crews were reluctant to extend themselves, even on a 187. Even when he pressed, emphasized the whodunit aspect, the ugliness, he got resistance. Finally, he hit upon something that pried cooperation and curses on the other end: the likelihood of news coverage. Cops were afraid of bad press. By 3 A.M., he'd come up with seven white girls in the right age range.

So what did he do, now? Get on the horn and wake up worried parents?

*Pardon me, Mrs. Jones, but did your daughter Amy ever show up? Because we've still got her listed as missing and are wondering if a sackful of tissue and viscera cooling off in a coroner's drawer just might be her.*

The only way to do it was preliminary phone contact followed by face-to-face interviews. Tomorrow, at a decent hour. Unless Schwinn had other ideas. Something else to correct him about.

He transcribed all the data from his pad onto report sheets, filled out the right forms, redrew the outline of the girl's body, summarized the MP calls, created a neat little pile of effort. Striding across the room to a bank of file cabinets, he opened a top drawer and pulled out one of several blue binders stored in a loose heap. Recycled binders: When cases were closed, the pages were removed and stapled, placed in a manila folder, and shipped over to the evidence room at Parker Center.

This particular blue book had seen better times, frayed around the edges with a brown stain on the front cover vaguely reminiscent of a wilting rose— some D's greasy lunch. Milo affixed a stickummed label to the cover.

Wrote nothing. Nothing to write.

He sat there thinking about the mutilated girl. Wondered what her name was and couldn't bring himself to substitute *Jane Doe*.

First thing tomorrow, he'd check out those seven girls, maybe get lucky and end up with a name.

A title for a brand-new murder book.

Bad dreams kept him up all night, and he was back at his desk by 6:45 A.M., the only detective in the room, which was just fine; he didn't even mind getting the coffee going.

By 7:20, he was calling families. MP number one was Sarah Jane Causlett, female cauc, eighteen, five-six, 121, last seen in Hollywood, buying dinner at the Oki-burger at Hollywood and Selma.

Ring, ring, ring. "Mrs. Causlett? Good morning, hope I'm not calling too early . . ."

By 9 A.M., he was finished. Three of the seven girls had returned home, and two others weren't missing at all, just players in divorce dramas who'd escaped to be with noncustodial parents. That left two sets of distraught parents, Mr. and Mrs. Estes in Mar Vista; Mr. and Mrs. Jacobs in Mid-City. Lots of anxiety, Milo withheld facts, steeled himself for the face-to-face.

By 9:30 a few detectives had arrived, but not

Schwinn, so Milo placed a scrawled note on
Schwinn's desk, left the station.

By 1 P.M., he was back where he started. A recent
picture of Misty Estes showed her to be substantially
obese with short curly hair. West L.A. Missing Persons had misrecorded her stats: 107 pounds instead
of 187. Oops, sorry. Milo left the tearful mother and
hypertensive father standing in the doorway of their
GI Bill bungalow.

Jessica Jacobs was approximately the right size, but
definitely not the girl on Beaudry: She had the lightest
of blue eyes, and the victim's had been deep brown.
Another clerical screwup, no one bothering to note
eye color in the Wilshire Division MP file.

He left the Jacobs house sweating and tired, found
a pay phone outside a liquor store at Third and
Wilton, got Schwinn on the line, and gave a lack-of-
progress report.

"Morning boy-o," said Schwinn. "Haul yourself
over here, there might be something."

"What?"

"Come on back."

When he got to the Homicide room, half the desks
were full, and Schwinn was balancing on two legs of
his chair, wearing a nice-looking navy suit, shiny
white-on-white shirt, gold tie, gold tie tack shaped
like a tiny fist. Leaning back precariously as he
chomped a burrito the size of a newborn baby.

"Welcome home, prodigious son."

"Yeah."

"You look like shit."

"Thanks."

"Don't mention it." Schwinn gave one of his corkscrew smiles. "So you learned about our excellent record keeping. Cops are the worst, boy-o. Hate to write and always make a mess out of it. We're talking barely literate."

Milo wondered about the extent of Schwinn's own education. The topic had never come up. The whole time they'd worked together, Schwinn had parceled out very few personal details.

"Clerical screwups are the fucking rule, boy-o. MP files are the worst, because MP knows it's a penny-ante outfit, most of the time the kid comes home, no one bothers to let them know."

"File it, forget it," said Milo, hoping agreement would shut him up.

"File it, *fuck* it. That's why I was in no big hurry to chase MP."

"You know best," said Milo.

Schwinn's eyes got hard. Milo said, "So what's interesting?"

"*Maybe* interesting," Schwinn corrected. "A source of mine picked up some rumors. Party on the Westside two days before the murder. Friday night, upper Stone Canyon—Bel Air."

"Rich kids."

"Filthy rich kids, probably using Daddy and Mommy's house. My source says there were kids from all over showing up, getting stoned, making noise. The source also knows a guy, has a daughter, went out with her friends, spent some time at the party, and never came home."

*Maybe interesting.*

Schwinn grinned and bit off a wad of burrito. Milo

had figured the guy for a late-sleeping pension-sniffing goldbrick and turned out the sonofabitch had been working overtime, doing a solo act, and *producing*. The two of them were partners in name only.

He said, "The father didn't report it to MP?"

Schwinn shrugged. "The father's a little bit . . . marginal."

"Lowlife?"

"Marginal," Schwinn repeated. Irritated, as if Milo was a poor student, kept getting it wrong. "Also, the girl's done this before—goes out partying, doesn't come home for a few days."

"If the girl's done it before, why would this be different?"

"Maybe it's not. But the girl fits stat-wise: sixteen, around five-seven, skinny, with dark hair, brown eyes, nice tight little body."

An appreciative tone had crept into Schwinn's voice. Milo pictured him with the source—some street letch, the source laying it on lasciviously. Hookers, pimps, perverts, Schwinn probably had a whole stable of lowlifes he could count on for info. And Milo had a master's degree . . .

"She's supposed to be cute," Schwinn went on. "No virgin, a wild kid. Also, at least one time before, she got herself in trouble. Hitchhiking on Sunset, got picked up by some scrote who raped her, tied her up, left her in an alley downtown. A juicehead found her, lucky for her he was just a bum, not a perv fixing to get himself some sloppy seconds. The girl never reported it officially, just told a friend, and the story made the rounds on the street."

"Sixteen years old, tied and raped and she doesn't report it?"

"Like I said, no virgin." Schwinn's hatchet jaw pulsed, and his Okie squint aimed at the ceiling. Milo knew he was holding back something.

"Is the source reliable?"

"Usually."

"Who?"

Schwinn's headshake was peevish. "Let's concentrate on the main thing: We got a girl who fits our vic's stats."

"Sixteen," said Milo, bothered.

Schwinn shrugged. "From what I've read— psychology articles—the human rope gets kinked up pretty early." He leaned back and took another big bite of burrito, wiped salsa verde from his mouth with the back of his hand, then gave the hand a lick. "You think that's true, boy-o? Think maybe she didn't report it 'cause she liked it?"

Milo covered his anger with a shrug of his own. "So what's next? Talk to the father?"

Schwinn righted his chair, swabbed his chin, this time with a paper napkin, stood abruptly, and walked out of the room, leaving Milo to follow.

Partners.

Outside, near the unmarked, Schwinn turned to him, smiling. "So tell me, how'd you sleep last night?"

Schwinn recited the address on Edgemont, and Milo started up the car.

"Hollywood, boy-o. A real-life Hollywood girl."

Over the course of the twenty-minute ride, he laid

out a few more details for Milo: The girl's name was
Janie Ingalls. A sophomore at Hollywood High, living with her father in a third-floor walk-up in a long-
faded neighborhood, just north of Santa Monica
Boulevard. Bowie Ingalls was a drunk who might or
might not be home. Society was going to hell in a
handbasket; even white folk were living like pigs.

The building was a clumsy pink thing with under-
sized windows and lumpy stucco. Twelve units was
Milo's guess: four flats to a floor, probably divided by
a narrow central corridor.

He parked, but Schwinn made no attempt to get
out, so the two of them just sat there, the engine running.

"Turn it off," said Schwinn.

Milo twisted the key and listened to street sounds.
Distant traffic from Santa Monica, a few bird trills,
someone unseen playing a power mower. The street
was poorly kept, litter sludging the gutters. He said,
"Besides being a juicehead, how's the father marginal?"

"One of those walking-around guys," said
Schwinn. "Name of Bowie Ingalls, does a little of
this, little of that. Rumor has it he ran slips for a nigger bookie downtown—how's that for a white man's
career? A few years ago, he was working as a messen-
ger at Paramount Studios, telling people he was in the
movie biz. He plays the horses, has a chickenshit
sheet, mostly drunk and disorderly, unpaid traffic
tickets. Two years ago he got pulled in for receiving
stolen property but never got charged. Small-time, all
around."

Details. Schwinn had found the time to pull Bowie Ingalls's record.

"Guy like that, and he's raising a kid," said Milo.

"Yeah, it's a cruel world, isn't it? Janie's mother was a stripper and a hype, ran off with some hippie musician when the kid was a baby, overdosed in Frisco."

"Sounds like you've learned a lot."

"That what you think?" Schwinn's voice got flinty, and his eyes were hard, again. Figuring Milo was being sarcastic? Milo wasn't sure he hadn't *meant* to be sarcastic.

"I've got a lot to learn," he said. "Wasting my time with those MP clowns. Meanwhile you're getting all this—"

"Don't lick my ass, son," said Schwinn, and suddenly the hatchet face was inches from Milo's and Milo could smell the Aqua Velva and the salsa verde. "I didn't *do* dick, and I don't *know* dick. And you did way *less* than dick."

"Hey, sorry if—"

"*Fuck* sorry, pal. You think this is some *game*? Like getting a master's degree, hand in your homework, and lick the teacher's ass and get your little ass-licking *grade*? You think *that's* what this is about?"

Talking way too fast for normal. What the hell had set him off?

Milo kept silent. Schwinn laughed bitterly, moved away, sat back so heavily against the seat that Milo's heavy body rocked. "Let me tell you, boy-o, that other shit we've been shoveling since I let you ride with me—niggers and pachucos offing each other and waiting around for us to pick 'em up and if we don't, no one gives a shit—you think that's what the 187 universe is all about?"

Milo's face was hot from jawline to scalp. He kept his mouth shut.

"This . . ." said Schwinn, pulling a letter-sized, baby blue envelope from an inside suit pocket and removing a stack of color photos. Twenty-four-hour photo lab logo. The Instamatic shots he'd snapped at Beaudry.

He fanned them out on his skinny lap, faceup, like fortune-teller's cards. Close-ups of the dead girl's bloody, scalped head. Intimate portraits of the lifeless face, splayed legs . . .

"*This*," he said, "is why we get paid. The other stuff *clerks* could handle."

The first seven murders had gotten Milo to think of himself as a clerk with a badge. He didn't dare agree. Agreement seemed to infuriate the sonofa—

"You thought you were gonna get some fun for yourself when you signed up to be a Big Bad Homicide Hero," said Schwinn. "Right?" Talking even faster, but managing to snap off each word. "Or maybe you heard that bullshit about Homicide being for intellectuals and you've got that master's degree and you thought hey, that's me! So tell me, this look *intellectual* to you?" Tapping a photo. "You think this can be figured out using brains?"

Shaking his head and looking as if he'd tasted something putrid, Schwinn hooked a fingernail under a corner of a photo and flicked.

*Plink, plink.*

Milo said, "Look, I'm just—"

"Do you have any idea how often something like

this actually gets closed? Those clowns in the Academy probably told you Homicide has a seventy, eighty percent solve rate, right? Well, that's *horseshit.* That's the stupid stuff—which should be a hundred percent it's so stupid, so big fucking deal, eighty percent. *Shit.*" He turned and spit out the window. Shifted back to Milo. "With *this*"—*plink plink*—"you're lucky to close four outta ten. Meaning most of the time you lose and the guy gets to do it again and he's saying 'Fuck you' to *you* just like he is to *her.*"

Schwinn freed his fingernail and began tapping the snapshot, blunt-edged index finger landing repetitively on the dead girl's crotch.

Milo realized he was holding his breath, had been doing it since Schwinn launched the tirade. His skin remained saturated with heat, and he wiped his face with one hand.

Schwinn smiled. "I'm pissing you off. Or maybe I'm scaring you. You do that—with the hand—when you're pissed off or scared."

"What's the point, Pierce?"

"The point is you said I learned a lot, and I didn't learn dick."

"I was just—"

"Don't *just* anything," said Schwinn. "There's no room for just, there's no room for bullshit. I don't need the brass sending me some . . . fly-by-night master's deg—"

"Fuck that," said Milo, letting out breath and rage. "I've been—"

"You've been watching me, checking me out, from the minute you started—"

"I've been hoping to learn something."

"For what?" said Schwinn. "So you can add up the brownie points, then move on to an ass-warming job with the brass. Boy-o, I know what you're about—"

Milo felt himself using his bulk. Moving closer to Schwinn, looming over the skinny man, his index finger pointing like a gun. "You don't know shi—"

Schwinn didn't yield. "I know assholes with master's degrees don't stick with *this.*" *Tap tap.* "I *know* I don't wanna waste my time working a whodunit with a suck-up intellectual who all he wants to do is climb the ladder. You got ambition, find yourself some suck-up job like Daryl Gates did, driving Chief Parker's car, one day that clown'll probably end up chief." *Taptaptap.* "*This* ain't career-building, muchacho. This is a *whodunit.* Get it? *This* likes to munch on your insides, then shit you out in pellets."

"You're wrong," said Milo. "About me."

"Am I?" Knowing smile.

*Ah,* thought Milo. *Here it comes. The crux.*

But Schwinn just sat there, grinning, tapping the photo.

Long silence. Then suddenly, as if someone had pulled the plug on him, the guy slumped heavily, looking defeated. "You have no *idea* what you're up against." He slipped the photos back in the envelope.

Milo thought: *If you hate the job, retire, asshole. Grab your pension two years early and waste the rest of your life growing tomatoes in some loser trailer park.*

Long, turgid moments passed.

Milo said, "Big whodunit, and we're sitting here?"

"What's the alternative, Sherlock?" said Schwinn,

hooking a thumb at the pink building. "We go in there and talk to this asshole and maybe his daughter's the one who got turned into shit, or she's not. One way, we've crawled an inch on a hundred-mile hike, the other way, we haven't even started. Either way we got nothing to be proud of."

# CHAPTER

# 8

Just as quickly as his mood had shifted, Schwinn bounded out of the car.

The guy was unstable, no question about it, Milo thought as he followed.

The front door was unlocked. Twelve mailboxes to the right. The layout was precisely as Milo had envisioned.

*Screw you, expert.*

Box Eleven was labeled INGALLS in smudged red ballpoint. They climbed the stairs, and Schwinn was out of breath by the time they reached the third floor. Tightening his tie knot, he pounded the door, and it opened a few seconds later.

The man who answered was bleary-eyed and skinny-fat.

All sharp bones and stick limbs and saggy sallow skin but with a melon gut. He wore a dirty yellow tank top and blue swim shorts. No hips or butt, and the shorts bagged under the swell of his pot. Not an ounce of extra flesh anywhere but his belly. But what he carried there was grotesque and Milo thought, *Pregnant.*

"Bowie Ingalls?" said Schwinn.

Two-second delay, then a small, squirrelly nod. Beery sweat poured out of the guy, and the sour smell wafted into the hallway.

Schwinn hadn't recited any physical stats on Ingalls—hadn't said anything at all by way of preparation. To Milo, Ingalls appeared in his midforties, with thick, wavy coarse black hair worn past his shoulders—too long and luxuriant for a guy his age— and five days of gray stubble that did nothing to mask his weak features. Where his eyes weren't pink they were jaundiced and unfocused. Deep brown irises, just like those of the dead girl.

Ingalls studied their badges. The guy's timing was off, like a clock with damaged works. He flinched, then grinned, said, "Whus up?" The words wheezed out on a cloud of hops and malt that mixed with the odors already saturated into the building's walls: mold and kerosene, the incongruous blessing of savory home cooking.

"Can we come in?" said Schwinn.

Ingalls had opened the door halfway. Behind him was dirt-colored furniture, heaps of rumpled clothes, take-out Chinese cartons, Bud empties.

Lots of empties, some crushed, some intact. Even at a good clip, the number of cans added up to more than one day of serious drinking.

A multiday bender. Unless the guy had company. Even *with* company, a focused juice-a-thon.

Guy's daughter goes missing for four days, he doesn't report it, holes up instead, sucking suds. Milo found himself entertaining the worst-case scenario: Daddy did it. Began scanning Ingalls's sallow face for anxiety, guilt, scratches, maybe that explained the delays . . .

But all he saw was confusion. Ingalls stood there, caught up in a booze-flummox.

"Sir," said Schwinn, using the word as an insult, the way only cops can, "can we come in?"

"Uh—yeah, sure—whu for?"

"Whu *for* your daughter."

Ingalls's eyes drooped. Not anxiety. Resignation. As in, *here we go again.* Preparing himself for a lecture on child-rearing.

"Whu, she cut school again? They call in the cops for that now?"

Schwinn smiled and moved to enter the apartment and Ingalls stepped aside, nearly stumbling. When the three of them were on the other side of the door, Schwinn closed it. He and Milo began the instinctive visual scan.

Off-white walls, brown deepening to black in the cracks and the corners. The entire front space was maybe fifteen feet square, a living room–dining area–kitchen combo, the kitchen counters crowded with more take-out boxes, used paper plates, empty soup cans. Two miserly windows on the facing wall were shuttered by yellow plastic blinds. A scabrous brown-gray sofa and a red plastic chair were both heaped with unwashed clothes and crumpled paper. Next to the chair, a stack of records tilted precariously. The Mothers of Invention's *Freak Out!* on top, a fifteen-year-old LP. Nearby was a cheap phonograph half-covered by a snot green bathrobe. An open doorway led to a dead-end wall.

A full view of the front room revealed even more beer cans.

"Where does Janie go to school, sir?" said Schwinn.

"Hollywood High. What kinda hassle she get herself into now?" Bowie Ingalls scratched an armpit and drew himself up to his full height. Trying to produce some fatherly indignation.

"When's the last time you saw her, sir?"

"Um . . . she was—she slept over a friend's."

"When, sir?" said Schwinn, still taking in the room. Cool, all business. No one watching him do the detective thing would've imagined his lunatic tirade five minutes ago.

Milo stood to the side, worked on his cool. His mind wanted to work, but his body wasn't giving up the anger planted by Schwinn's outburst; heart still racing, face still hot. Despite the importance of the task at hand, he kept entertaining himself with images of Schwinn falling on his ass—hoist on his own petard, the self-righteous fucker—busted *in flagrante* with Tonya or some other "source." That brought a smile to Milo's brain. Then a question arose: If Schwinn didn't trust him, why had he risked doing Tonya right in front of him? Maybe the guy was just nuts . . . he shook all that off and returned to Bowie Ingalls's face. Still no fear, just maddening dullness.

"Um . . . Friday night," Ingalls said, as if guessing. "You can sit down if you want."

There was only one place to sit in the damned sty. A man-sized clearing among the garbage on the couch. Ingalls's dozing spot. Appetizing.

"No, thanks," said Schwinn. He had his pad out

now. Milo waited a few moments before producing his. Not wanting to be part of some Ike-and-Mike vaudeville routine. "So Janie slept at a friend's Friday night."

"Yeah. Friday."

"Four days ago." Schwinn's gold Parker ballpoint was out, and he scrawled.

"Yeah. She does it all the time."

"Sleeps over at a friend's?"

"She's sixteen," said Ingalls, whining a bit.

"What's the friend's name? The one from Friday night."

Ingalls's tongue rolled around his left cheek. "Linda . . . no—*Me*linda."

"Last name?"

Blank stare.

"You don't know Melinda's last name?"

"Don't like the little slut," said Ingalls. "Bad influence. Don't like her coming around."

"Melinda's a bad influence on Janie?"

"Yeah. You know."

"Gets Janie in trouble," said Schwinn.

"You know," said Ingalls. "Kids. Doing stuff."

Milo wondered what could possibly offend a scrote like Ingalls.

Schwinn said, "Stuff."

"Yeah."

"Such as?"

"You know," Ingalls insisted. "Cutting school, running around."

"Dope?"

"I dunno about that."

"Hmm," said Schwinn, writing. "So Melinda's a

bad influence on Janie but you let Janie sleep over Melinda's house."

"*Let?*" said Ingalls, coughing. "You got kids?"

"Haven't been blessed."

"Figures you ask me that. Nowadays, kids don't get *let* anything. They do whatever the hell they want to. Can't even get her to tell me where she's going. Or to stay in school. I tried dropping her off, personally, but she just went in, waited till I was gone, and left. That's why I figured this was about school. What is it about, anyway? She in trouble?"

"You've had trouble with Janie before?"

"No," said Ingalls. "Not really. Like I said, just school and running around. Being gone for a few days. But she always comes back. Let me tell you, man, you can't control 'em. Once the hippies got in and took over the city, forget it. Her mother was a hippie back in the hippie days. Hippie junkie slut, ran out on us, left me with Janie."

"Janie into drugs?"

"Not around here," said Ingalls. "She knows better than that." He blinked several times, grimaced, trying to clear his head and not succeeding. "What's this about? What'd she do?"

Ignoring the question, Schwinn kept writing. Then: "Hollywood High . . . what year's she in?"

"Second year."

"Sophomore."

Another delayed-reaction nod from Ingalls. How many of the cans had been consumed this morning?

"Sophomore." Schwinn copied that down. "When's her birthday?"

"Um . . . March," said Ingalls. "March . . . um . . . ten."

"She was sixteen last March ten."

"Yeah."

Sixteen-and-a-half-year-old sophomore, thought Milo. A year behind. Borderline intelligence? Some kind of learning problem? Yet another factor that had propelled her toward victimhood? If she was the one . . .

He glanced at Schwinn but Schwinn was still writing and Milo hazarded a question of his own: "School's hard for Janie, huh?"

Schwinn's eyebrows rose for a second, but he kept making notes.

"She hates it," said Ingalls. "Can barely read. That's why she hated to—" The bloodshot eyes filled with fear. "What's going on? What'd she do?"

Focused on Milo, now. Looking to Milo for an answer, but that was one ad lib Milo wasn't going to risk, and Ingalls shifted his attention back to Schwinn. "C'mon, what's going on, man? What'd she do?"

"Maybe nothing," said Schwinn, producing the blue envelope. "Maybe something was done to her."

He fanned out the snaps again, stretching his arm and offering Ingalls the display.

"Huh?" said Ingalls, not moving. Then: "No."

Calmly, no inflection. Milo thought: Okay, it wasn't her, false lead, good for him, bad for us, they'd accomplished nothing, Schwinn was right. As usual. The pompous bastard, he'd be gloating, the remainder of the shift would be unbearable—

But Schwinn continued to hold the pictures steady, and Bowie Ingalls continued to stare at them.

"No," Ingalls repeated. He made a grab for the pictures, not a serious attempt, just a pathetic stab. Schwinn held firm, and Ingalls stepped away from the horror, pressing his hands to the sides of his head. Stamping his foot hard enough to make the floor quake.

Suddenly, he grabbed his melon-belly, bent over as if seized by cramps. Stamped again, howled, *"No!"*

Kept howling.

Schwinn let him rant for a while, then eased him over to the clearing on the couch, and told Milo, "Get him some fortification."

Milo found an unopened Bud, popped the top, held it to Ingalls's lips, but Ingalls shook his head. "No, no, no. Get that the fuck away from me."

The guy lives in a booze-haze but won't medicate himself when he sinks to the bottom. Milo supposed that passed for dignity.

He and Schwinn stood there for what seemed to be an eternity. Schwinn serene—used to this. Enjoying it?

Finally, Ingalls looked up. "Where?" he said. "Who?"

Schwinn gave him the basic details, talking quietly. Ingalls moaned through the entire recitation.

"Janie, Janie—"

"What can you tell us that would help us?" said Schwinn.

"Nothing. What could I tell . . . ?" Ingalls shuddered. Shivered. Crossed skinny arms over his chest. "That—who would—oh, God . . . *Janie* . . ."

"Tell us something," pressed Schwinn. "Anything. Help us."

"What . . . I don't know . . . She didn't—since she was fourteen, she's basically been gone, using this place as a crash pad but always gone, telling me to fuck off, mind my own business. Half the time, she ain't here, see what I'm sayin'?"

"Sleeping at friends' houses," said Schwinn. "Melinda, other friends."

"Whatever . . . oh God, I can't believe this. . . ." Tears filled Ingalls's eyes, and Schwinn was there with a snow-white hankie. PS monogram in gold thread on a corner. The guy talked despair and pessimism, but offered his own starched linen to a drunk, for the sake of the job.

"Help me," he whispered to Ingalls. "For Janie."

"I would . . . I don't know—she . . . I . . . we didn't talk. Not since . . . she used to be my kid, but then she didn't want to be my kid, telling me to fuck off all the time. I'm not saying I was any big deal as a daddy, but still, without me, Janie would've . . . she turned thirteen and all of a sudden she didn't appreciate anything. Started going out all hours, the school didn't give a shit. Janie never went, no one from the school ever called me, not one time."

"You call them?"

Ingalls shook his head. "What's the point? Talking to people who don't give a shit. I'da called, they'da probably sent cops over and busted me for something, child neglect, whatever. I was busy, man. Working—I used to work at Paramount Studios."

"Oh, yeah?" said Schwinn.

"Yeah. Publicity department. Information transfer."

"Janie interested in the movies?"

"Nah," said Ingalls. "Anything I was into she *wasn't* into."

"What was she into?"

"Nothing. Running around."

"This friend, Melinda. If Janie never told you where she was going, how do you know she was with Melinda Friday night?"

"Because I seen her with Melinda on Friday."

"What time?"

"Around six. I was sleeping, and Janie busts in to get some clothes, I wake up, by the time I'm sitting up, she's heading out the door, and I look out there." He jabbed a thumb at the shuttered windows. "I seen her walking away with Melinda."

"Walking which way?"

"That way." Hooking his finger north. Toward Sunset, maybe Hollywood Boulevard, if the girls had kept going.

"Anyone else with them?"

"No, just the two of them."

"Walking, not driving," said Schwinn.

"Janie didn't have no license. I got one car, and it barely drives. No way was I gonna—she didn't care, anyway. Got around by hitching. I told her about that—I used to hitch, back when you could do it, but now, with all the—you think that's what happened? She hitched and some . . . oh, God . . ."

Unaware of Janie's downtown rape? If so, the guy

was being truthful about one thing: Janie had been lost to him for a long time.

"Some what?" said Schwinn.

"Some—you know," moaned Ingalls. "Getting picked up—some stranger."

The death snaps were back in the envelope, but Schwinn had kept the envelope in full view. Now he waved it inches from Ingalls's face. "I'd say, sir, that only a stranger would do something like this. Unless you have some other idea?"

"Me? No," said Ingalls. "She was like her mother. Didn't talk—gimme that beer."

When the can was empty, Schwinn waved the envelope again. "Let's get back to Friday. Janie came home to get clothes. What was she wearing?"

Ingalls thought. "Jeans and a T-shirt—red T-shirt . . . and those crazy black shoes with those heels—platform heels. She was *carrying* her party clothes."

"Party clothes."

"When I woke up and saw her going out the door, I could see part of what she had in the bag."

"What kind of bag?"

"Shopping bag. White—Zody's, probably, 'cause that's where she shops. She always stuffed her party stuff inside shopping bags."

"What did you see in the bag?"

"Red halter the size of a Band-Aid. I always told her it was hooker shit, she should throw it out, used to threaten her I'd throw it out."

"But you didn't."

"No," said Ingalls. "What woulda been the point?"

"A red halter," said Schwinn. "What else?"

"That's all I saw. Probably a skirt, one of those microminis, that's all she buys. The shoes she already had on."

"Black with big heels."

"Shiny black," said Ingalls. "Patent leather. Those crazy heels, I kept telling her she'd fall and break her neck."

"Party outfit," said Schwinn, copying.

Red-and-black party outfit, thought Milo. Remembering something that had gone round in high school, boys sitting around pontificating, pointing with glee: Red and black on Fridays meant a girl put out all the way. Him, laughing along, pretending to care . . .

Bowie Ingalls said, "Except for the jeans and T-shirts, that's all she buys. Party stuff."

"Speaking of which," said Schwinn, "let's take a look at her closet."

The rest of the apartment was two cell-sized bedrooms separated by a windowless bathroom stale with flatulence.

Schwinn and Milo glanced into Bowie Ingalls's sleep chamber as they passed. A queen-size mattress took up most of the floor. Unwashed sheets were pulled half-off, and they puddled on cheap carpeting. A tiny TV threatened to topple from a pressed-wood bureau. More Bud empties.

Janie's room was even smaller, with barely enough space for a single mattress and a nightstand of the same synthetic wood. Cutouts from teen magazines were taped to the walls, mounted at careless angles. A single, muddy-looking stuffed koala slumped on the nightstand, next to a soft pack of Kents and a half-empty box of Luden's cough drops. The room was so cramped that the mattress prevented the closet door from opening all the way, and Schwinn had to contort to get a look inside.

He winced, stepped out, and told Milo, "You do it."

Milo's size made the task excruciating, but he obeyed.

Zody's was a cut-rate barn. Even at their prices, Janie Ingalls hadn't assembled much of a wardrobe. On the dusty floor sat one pair of tennis shoes, size 8, next to red Thom McAn platform sandals and white plastic boots with see-through plastic soles. Two pairs of size S jeans were carelessly hung in the closet, one faded denim with holes that could've been genuine wear or contrivance, the other denim patchwork, both made in Taiwan. Four ribbed, snug-fit T-shirts with bias-cut sleeves, a floral cotton blouse with moth wounds pocking the breast pocket, three shiny, polyester halter tops not much bigger than the hankie Schwinn had offered to Ingalls—peacock blue, black, pearlescent white. A red sweatshirt emblazoned *Hollywood* in puffy gold letters, a black plastic shortie jacket pretending to be leather, cracking like an old lady's face.

On the top shelf were bikini underpants, bras, panty hose, more dust. Everything stank of tobacco. Only a few pockets to search. Other than grit and lint and a Doublemint wrapper, Milo found nothing. Such a *blank* existence—not unlike his own apartment, he hadn't bothered to furnish much since arriving in L.A., had never been sure he'd be staying.

He searched the rest of the room. The magazine posters were the closest thing to personal possessions. No diary or date book or photographs of friends. If Janie had ever called this dump home, she'd changed her mind sometime ago. He wondered if she had some other place of refuge—a crash pad, a sanctuary, somewhere she *kept* stuff.

He checked under the bed, found dirt. When he extricated himself, his neck killed and his shoulders throbbed.

Schwinn and Ingalls were back in the front room, and Milo stopped to check out the bathroom, compressing his nostrils to block out the stench, examining the medicine cabinet. All over-the-counter stuff—painkillers, laxatives, diarrhea remedies, antacids—a host of antacids. Something eating at Bowie Ingalls's gut? Guilt or just alcohol?

Milo found himself craving a drink.

When he joined Schwinn and Ingalls, Ingalls was slumped on the couch, looking disoriented, saying, "What do I do now?"

Schwinn stood away from the guy, detached. No more use for Ingalls. "There'll be some procedures to go through—identification, filling out forms. Identification can wait till after the autopsy. We may have more questions for you."

Ingalls looked up. "About what?"

Schwinn handed Ingalls his card. "If you think of anything, give a call."

"I already told you everything."

Milo said, "Was there anywhere else Janie mighta crashed?"

"Like what?"

"Like a crash pad. Somewhere kids go."

"I dunno where kids go. Dunno where my own kid goes, so how would I know?"

"Okay, thanks. Sorry for your loss, Mr. Ingalls."

Schwinn motioned Milo to the door, but when they got there, he turned back to Ingalls. "One more thing: What does Melinda look like?"

Basic question, thought Milo, but he hadn't thought to ask it. Schwinn had, but he orchestrated it, timed everything. The guy was nuts but miles ahead of him.

"Short, big tits—built big—kinda fat. Blond hair, real long, straight."

"Voluptuous," said Schwinn, enjoying the word.

"Whatever."

"And she's Janie's age?"

"Maybe a little older," said Ingalls.

"A sophomore, too?"

"I dunno what she is."

"Bad influence," said Schwinn.

"Yeah."

"Do you have a picture of Janie? Something we could show around?"

"I'd have to have one, wouldn't I?" said Bowie, making it sound like the answer to an oral exam. Pulling himself to his feet, he stumbled to his bedroom, returned moments later with a three-by-five snap.

A dark-haired child around ten years old, wearing a sleeveless dress and staring at a five-foot-tall Mickey Mouse. Mickey giving that idiot grin, the kid unimpressed—scared, actually. No way to connect this child to the outrage on Beaudry.

"Disneyland," said Ingalls.

"You took Janie there?" said Milo, trying to imagine that.

"Nah, it was a school trip. They got a group discount."

Schwinn returned the photo to Ingalls. "I was thinking in terms of something more recent."

"I should have something," said Ingalls, "but hell if I can find anything—if I do, I'll call you."

"I noticed," said Milo, "that there was no diary in Janie's room."

"You say so."

"You never saw a diary or a date book—a photo album?"

Ingalls shook his head. "I stayed out of Janie's stuff, but she wouldn't have any of that. Janie didn't like to write. Writing was hard for her. Her mother was like that, too: never really learned to read. I tried to teach Janie. The school didn't do shit."

Papa Juicehead huddled with Janie, tutoring. Hard to picture.

Schwinn frowned—he'd lost patience with Milo's line of questioning and gave the doorknob a sharp twist. "Afternoon, Mr. Ingalls."

As the door closed, Ingalls cried out: "She was my kid."

"What a stupid asshole," said Schwinn, as they headed to Hollywood High. "Stupid parents, stupid kid. Genes. That's what you were getting at, right, with those questions about school?"

"I was thinking learning problems coulda made her an easier victim," said Milo.

Schwinn grumbled, "Anyone can be a victim."

* * *

The school was an ugly pile of gray-brown stucco that filled a block on the north side of Sunset just west of Highland. As impersonal as an airport, and Milo felt the curse of futility the moment his feet touched down on the campus. He and Schwinn walked past what seemed to be thousands of kids—every one of them bored, spaced, surly. Smiles and laughter were aberrations, and any eye contact directed at the detectives was hostile.

They asked directions of a teacher, got the same icy reception, not much better at the principal's office. As Schwinn talked to a secretary, Milo studied girls walking through the sweaty corridor. Tight or minimal clothes and hooker makeup seemed to be the mode, all those freshly developed bodies promising something they might not be able to deliver, and he wondered how many potential Janies were out there.

The principal was at a meeting downtown, and the secretary routed them to the vice principal for operations, who sent them farther down the line to the guidance office. The counselor they spoke to was a pretty young woman named Ellen Sato, tiny, Eurasian, with long, side-winged, blond-tipped hair. The news of Janie's murder made her face crumple, and Schwinn took advantage of it by pressing her with questions.

Useless. She'd never heard of Janie, finally admitted she'd been on the job for less than a month. Schwinn kept pushing and she disappeared for a while, then returned with bad news: no INGALLS, J. files on record for any guidance sessions or disciplinary actions.

The girl was a habitual truant, but hadn't entered

the system. Bowie Ingalls had been right about one thing: No one cared.

The poor kid had never had any moorings, thought Milo, remembering his own brush with truancy: back when his family still lived in Gary and his father was working steel, making good money, feeling like a breadwinner. Milo was nine, had been plagued by terrible dreams since the summer—visions of men. One dreary Monday, he got off the school bus and instead of entering the school grounds just kept walking aimlessly, placing one foot in front of the other. Ending up at a park, where he sat on a bench like a tired old man. All day. A friend of his mother spotted him, reported him. Mom had been perplexed; Dad, always action-oriented, knew just what to do. Out came the strap. Ten pounds of oily ironworker's belt. Milo hadn't sat comfortably for a long, long time.

Yet another reason to hate the old man. Still, he'd never repeated the offense, ended up graduating with good grades. Despite the dreams. And all that followed. Certain his father would've killed him if he knew what was *really* going on.

So he made plans at age nine: *You need to get away from these people.*

Now he mused: *Maybe I was the lucky one.*

"Okay," Schwinn was telling Ellen Sato, "so you people don't know much about her—"

The young woman was on the verge of tears. "I'm sorry, sir, but as I said, I just . . . what happened to her?"

"Someone killed her," said Schwinn. "We're looking for a friend of hers, probably a student here, also. Melinda, sixteen or seventeen. Long blond hair.

Vo*lup*tuous." Cupping his hands in front of his own, scrawny chest.

Sato's ivory skin pinkened. "Melinda's a common name—"

"How about a look at your student roster?"

"The roster . . ." Sato's graceful hands fluttered. "I could find a yearbook for you."

"You have no student roster?"

"I—I know we have class lists, but they're over in V.P. Sullivan's office and there are forms to be filled out. Okay, sure, I'll go look. In the meantime, I know where the yearbooks are. Right here." Pointing to a closet.

"Great," said Schwinn, without graciousness.

"Poor Janie," said Sato. "Who would do such a thing?"

"Someone *evil*, ma'am. Anyone come to mind?"

"Oh, heavens no—I wasn't . . . let me go get that list."

The two detectives sat on a bench in the counseling office waiting room, flipping through the yearbooks, ignoring the scornful eyes of the students who came and went. Copying down the names of every Caucasian Melinda, freshmen included, because who knew how accurate Bowie Ingalls was about age. Not limiting the count to blondes, either, because hair dye was a teenage-girl staple.

Milo said, "What about light-skinned Mexicans?"

"Nah," said Schwinn. "If she was a greaser, Ingalls would've mentioned it."

"Why?"

"Because he doesn't like her, would've loved to add another bad point to the list."

Milo returned to checking out young white faces. The end product: eighteen possibles.

Schwinn regarded the list and scowled. "Names but no numbers. We'll still need a fucking roster to track her down."

Talking low but his tone was unmistakable and the receptionist a few feet away looked over and frowned.

"Howdy," said Schwinn, raising his voice and grinning at the woman furiously. She flinched and returned to her typewriter.

Milo looked up Janie Ingalls's freshman photo. No list of extracurricular activities. Huge, dark hair teased with abandon over a pretty oval face turned ghostly by slathers of makeup and ghoulish eye shadow. The image before him was neither the ten-year-old hanging with Mickey nor the corpse atop the freeway ramp. So many identities for a sixteen-year-old kid. He asked the receptionist to make a photocopy, and she agreed, grudgingly. Staring first at the picture.

"Know her, ma'am?" Milo asked her as pleasantly as possible.

"No. Here you go. It didn't come out too good. Our machine needs adjusting."

Ellen Sato returned, freshly made-up, weak-eyed, forcing a smile. "How'd we do?"

Schwinn bounded up quickly, was in her face, bullying her with body language, beaming that same hostile grin. "Oh, just great, ma'am." He brandished the list of eighteen names. "Now how about introducing us to these lovely ladies?"

Rounding up the Melindas took another forty minutes. Twelve out of eighteen girls were in attendance that day, and they marched in looking supremely bored. Only a couple were vaguely aware of Janie Ingalls's existence, none admitted to being a close friend or knowing anyone who was, none seemed to be holding back.

Not much curiosity, either, about why they'd been called in to talk to cops. As if a police presence was the usual thing at Hollywood High. Or they just didn't care.

One thing *was* clear: Janie hadn't made her mark on campus. The girl who was the most forthcoming ended up in Milo's queue. Barely blond, not-at-all voluptuous Melinda Kantor. "Oh yeah, her. She's a stoner, right?"

"Is she?" he said.

The girl shrugged. She had a long, pretty face, a bit equine. Two-inch nails glossed aqua, no bra.

Milo said, "Does she hang around with other stoners?"

"Uh-uh, she's not a social stoner—more like a loner stoner."

"A loner stoner."

"Yeah."

"Which means . . ."

The girl shot him a *you-are-a-prime-lame-o* look. "She run away or something?"

"Something like that."

"Well," said Melinda Kantor, "maybe she's over on the Boulevard."

"Hollywood Boulevard?"

The resultant smirk said, *Another stupid question,* and Milo knew he was losing her. "The boulevard's where the loner stoners go."

Now Melinda Kantor was regarding him as if he were brain-dead. "I was just making a *suggestion.* What'd she do?"

"Maybe nothing."

"Yeah, right," said the girl. "Weird."

"What is?"

"Usually they send over narcs who are young and cute."

Ellen Sato produced addresses and phone numbers for the six absent Melindas, and Milo and Schwinn spent the rest of the day paying house calls.

The first four girls lived in smallish but tidy single homes on Hollywood's border with the Los Feliz district and were out sick. Melindas Adams, Greenberg, Jordan were in bed with the flu, Melinda Hohlmeister had been felled by an asthma attack. All four mothers were in attendance, all were freaked out by the drop-in, but each allowed the detectives access. The previous generation still respected—or feared—authority.

Melinda Adams was a tiny, platinum-haired, fourteen-year-old freshman who looked eleven and had a little kid's demeanor to match. Melinda Jordan was a skinny fifteen-year-old brunette with a frighteningly runny nose and vengeful acne. Greenberg was blond and long-haired and somewhat chesty. Both she and her mother had thick, almost impenetrable accents—

recent immigrants from Israel. Science and math books were spread over her bed. When the detectives had stepped in, she'd been underlining text in yellow marker, had no idea who Janie Ingalls was. Melinda Hohlmeister was a shy, chubby, stuttering, homely kid with short, corn-colored ringlets, a straight A average, and an audible wheeze.

No response to Janie's name from any of them.

No answer at Melinda Van Epps's big white contemporary house up in the hills. A woman next door picking flowers volunteered that the family was in Europe, had been gone for two weeks. The father was an executive with Standard Oil, the Van Eppses took all five kids out of school all the time for travel, provided tutors, lovely people.

No reply, either, at Melinda Waters's shabby bungalow on North Gower. Schwinn knocked hard because the bell was taped over and labeled "Broken."

"Okay, leave a note," he told Milo. "It'll probably be bullshit, too."

Just as Milo was slipping the *please-call-us* memo and his card through the mail slot, the door swung open.

The woman who stood there could have been Bowie Ingalls's spiritual sister. Fortyish, thin but flabby, wearing a faded brown housedress. She had a mustard complexion, wore her peroxided hair pinned back carelessly. Confused blue eyes, no makeup, cracked lips. That furtive look.

"Mrs. Waters?" said Milo.

"I'm Eileen." Cigarette voice. "What is it?"

Schwinn showed her the badge. "We'd like to talk to Melinda."

Eileen Waters's head retracted, as if he'd slapped her. "About what?"

"Her friend, Janie Ingalls."

"Oh. Her," said Waters. "What'd she do?"

"Someone killed her," said Schwinn. "Did a right sloppy job of it. Where's Melinda?"

Eileen Waters's parched lips parted, revealing uneven teeth coated with yellow scum. She'd relied upon suspiciousness as a substitute for dignity and now, losing both, she slumped against the doorjamb. "Oh my God."

"Where's Melinda?" demanded Schwinn.

Waters shook her head, lowered it. "Oh, God, oh God."

Schwinn took her arm. His voice remained firm. "Where's Melinda?"

More headshakes, and when Eileen Waters spoke again her voice was that of another woman: timid, chastened. Reduced.

She began crying. Finally stopped. "Melinda never came home, I haven't seen her since *Friday*."

## CHAPTER 9

The Waters household was a step up from Bowie Ingalls's flop, furnished with old, ungainly furniture that might've been hand-me-downs from some upright Midwestern homestead. Browning doilies on the arms of overstuffed chairs said someone had once cared. Ashtrays were everywhere, filled with gray dust and butts, and the air felt sooty. No beer empties, but Milo noticed a quarter-full bottle of Dewar's on a kitchen counter next to a jam jar packed with something purple. Every drape was drawn, plunging the house into perpetual evening. The sun could be punishing when your body subsisted on ethanol.

Either Schwinn had developed an instant dislike for Eileen Waters or his bad mood had intensified or he had a genuine reason for riding her hard. He sat her down on a sofa, and began peppering her with questions.

She did nothing to defend herself other than chain-smoke Parliaments, was easy with the confessions:

Melinda was wild, had been wild for a long time, had fought off any attempts at discipline. Yes, she used drugs—marijuana, for sure. Eileen had found roaches in her pockets, wasn't sure about anything harder, but wasn't denying the possibility.

"What about Janie Ingalls?" asked Schwinn.

"You kidding? She's probably the one introduced Melinda to dope."

"Why's that?"

"That kid was stoned all the time."

"How old's Melinda?"

"Seventeen."

"What year in school?"

"Eleventh grade—I know Janie's in tenth but just because Melinda's older doesn't mean she was the instigator. Janie was street-smart. I'm sure Janie's the one got Melinda into grass . . . Lord, where could she *be*?"

Milo thought back to his search of Janie's room: no evidence of dope, not even rolling paper or a pipe.

"Melinda and Janie were a perfect pair," Waters was saying. "Neither of them gave a damn about school, they cut all the time."

"What'd you do about it?"

The woman laughed. "Right." Then the fear came back. "Melinda will come back, she always does."

"In what way was Janie streetwise?" said Schwinn.

"You know," said Waters. "You can just tell. Like she'd been around."

"Sexually?"

"I assume. Melinda was basically a good girl."

"Janie spend much time here?"

"No. Mostly she'd pick up Melinda, and they'd be off."

"That the case last Friday?"

"Dunno."

"What do you mean?"

"I was out shopping. Came home, and Melinda was gone. I could tell she'd been here because she left her underwear on the floor and some food out in the kitchen."

"Food for one?"

Waters thought. "One Popsicle wrapper and a Pepsi can—I guess."

"So the last time you saw Melinda was Friday morning, but you don't know if Janie came by to pick her up."

Waters nodded. "She claimed she was going to school, but I don't think so. She had a bag full of clothes, and when I said, 'What's all that?' she said she was going to some party that night, might not be coming home. We got into a hassle about that, but what could I do? I wanted to know where the party was but all she told me was it was fancy, on the West-side."

"Where on the Westside?"

"I just told you, she wouldn't say." The woman's face twitched. "Fancy party. Rich kids. She said that a bunch of times. Told me I had nothing to worry about."

She looked to Schwinn, then Milo, for reassurance, got two stone faces.

"Fancy Westside party," said Schwinn. "So maybe Beverly Hills—or Bel Air."

"I guess . . . I asked her how she was getting all the way over there, she said she'd find a way. I told her not to hitch, and she said she wouldn't."

"You don't like her hitching."

"Would you? Standing there on Sunset, thumbing,

any kind of pervert . . ." She stopped, went rigid. "Where was—where'd you find Janie?"

"Near downtown."

Waters relaxed. "So there you go, the complete opposite direction. Melinda wasn't with her. Melinda was over on the Westside."

Schwinn's slit eyes made the merest turn toward Milo. Bowie Ingalls had seen Melinda pick Janie up on Friday, watched the two girls walking north toward Thumb Alley. But no reason to get into that, now.

"Melinda'll come back," said Waters. "Sometimes she does that. Stays away. She always comes back."

"Sometimes," said Schwinn. "Like once a week?"

"No, nothing like that—just once in a while."

"And how long does she stay away?"

"A night," said Waters, sagging and trying to calm herself with a twenty-second pull on her cigarette. Her hand shook. Confronting the fact that this was Melinda's longest absence.

Then she perked up. "One time she stayed away two days. Went up to see her father. He's in the Navy, used to live in Oxnard."

"Where's he live now?"

"Turkey. He's at a naval base, there. Shipped out two months ago."

"How'd Melinda get to Oxnard?"

Eileen Waters chewed her lip. "Hitched. I'm not going to tell him. Even if I could reach him in Turkey, he'd just start in with the accusations . . . and that bitch of his."

"Second wife?" said Schwinn.

"His whore," spat Waters. "Melinda hated her. Melinda will come home."

Further questioning was futile. The woman knew nothing more about the "fancy Westside party," kept harping on the downtown murder site as clear proof Melinda hadn't been with Janie. They pried a photo of Melinda out of her. Unlike Bowie Ingalls, she'd maintained an album, and though Melinda's teen years were given short shrift, the detectives had a page of snaps from which to choose.

Bowie Ingalls hadn't been fair to Melinda Waters. Nothing chubby about the girl's figure, she was beautifully curvy with high, round breasts and a tiny waist. Straight blond hair hung to her rear. Kiss-me lips formed a heartbreaking smile.

"Looks like Marilyn, doesn't she?" said her mother. "Maybe one day, she'll be a movie star."

Driving back to the station, Milo said, "How long before her body shows up?"

"Who the fuck knows?" said Schwinn, studying Melinda's picture. "From the looks of this, maybe Janie was the appetizer and this one was the main dish. Look at those tits. That'd give him something to play with for a while. Yeah, I can see him holding on to this one for a while."

He pocketed the photo.

Milo envisioned a torture chamber. The blond girl nude, shackled . . . "So what do we do about finding her?"

"Nothing," said Schwinn. "If she's already dead, we have to wait till she shows up. If he's still got her, he's not gonna tell us."

"What about that Westside party?"

"What about it?"

"We could put the word out with West L.A., the sheriffs, Beverly Hills PD. Sometimes parties get wild, the blues go out on a nuisance call."

"So what?" said Schwinn. "We show up at some rich asshole's door, say, 'Excuse me, are you cutting up this kid?'" He sniffed, coughed, produced his bottle of decongestant, and swigged. "Shit, Waters's dump was dusty. All-American mom, another poor excuse for an adult. Who knows if there even *was* a party."

"Why wouldn't there be?"

"Because kids lie to their parents." Schwinn swiveled toward Milo. "What's with all these fucking questions? You thinking of going to law school?"

Milo held his tongue, and the rest of the ride was their usual joy-fest. A block from the station, Schwinn said, "You wanna go snooping for Westside nuisance calls, be my guest, but I think Blondie was lying to Mommy like she always did because a fancy Westside party was exactly the kind of thing that would calm the old lady down. Hundred to one Blondie and Janie were fixing to thumb the Strip, score some dope, maybe trade blow jobs for it, or whatever. They got into the wrong set of wheels and ended up downtown. Janie was too stupid to learn from her past experience—or like I said, maybe she liked being tied up. She was a stoner. Both of them probably were."

"Your source mentioned a Westside party."

"Street talk's like watermelon, you got to pick around the seeds. The main thing is Janie was *found* downtown. And chances are Melinda's somewhere around there, too, if a scrote got her and finished with her. For all we know, he kept her in the trunk while he was setting up Janie on Beaudry. Got back on the freeway, he could be in Nevada by now."

He shook his head. "Stupid kids. Two of them thought they had the world in their sweet little hands, and the world upped and bit 'em."

Back at the station, Schwinn collected his things from his desk and walked off without a word to Milo. Not even bothering to sign out. No one noticed: None of the detectives paid much attention to Schwinn, period.

An outcast, Milo realized. *Did they stick me with him by coincidence?*

Pushing all that aside, he played phone poker until well after dark. Contacting every police entity west of Hollywood Division in search of 415 party calls. Throwing in rent-a-cop outfits, too: The Bel Air Patrol, and other private firms that covered Beverlywood, Cheviot Hills, Pacific Palisades. The privates turned out to be the worst to deal with—no one was willing to talk without supervisory clearance and Milo had to leave his name and badge number, wait for callbacks that probably wouldn't happen.

He kept going, casting his net to Santa Monica and beyond, even including the southern edge of Ventura County, because Melinda Waters had once hitched PCH to Oxnard to see her father. And kids flocked to the beach for parties—he'd spent many a sleepless night driving up and down the coast highway, spotting bonfires that sparked the tide, the faint silhouettes of couples. Wondering what it would be like to have someone.

Four hours of work resulted in two measly hits—either L.A. had turned sleepy, or no one was complaining about noise anymore.

Two big zeros: An eye surgeon's fiftieth birthday party on Roxbury Drive in Beverly Hills had evoked a Friday midnight complaint from a cranky neighbor.

"Kids? No, don't think so," laughed the BH desk officer. "We're talking black tie, all that good stuff. Lester Lanin's orchestra playing swing and still someone bitched. There's always some killjoy, right?"

The second call was a Santa Monica item: A bar mitzvah on Fifth Street north of Montana had been closed down just after 2 A.M., after rambunctious thirteen-year-olds began setting off firecrackers.

Milo put the phone down and stretched. His ears burned and his neck felt like dry ice. Schwinn's voice was an obnoxious mantra in his head as he left the station just before 1 A.M.

*Told you so, asshole. Told you so, asshole.*

He drove to a bar—a straight one on Eighth Street, not far from the Ambassador Hotel. He'd passed it several times, a shabby-looking place on the ground floor of an old brick apartment building that had seen better days. The few patrons drinking this late were past their prime, too, and his entrance lowered the median age by a few decades. Mel Torme on tape loop, scary-looking toothpicked shrimp and bowls full of cracker medley decorated the cloudy bar top. Milo downed a few shots and beers, kept his head down, left, and drove north to Santa Monica Boulevard, cruising Boystown for a while but didn't even wrestle with temptation: Tonight the male hookers looked predatory, and he realized he wanted to be with no one, not even himself. When he reached his apartment, images of Eileen Waters's torment had returned to plague him, and he pulled down a bottle of Jim Beam from a kitchenette cupboard. Tired but wired. Removing his clothes was an ordeal, and the sight of his pitiful, white body made him close his eyes.

He lay in bed, wishing the darkness was more complete. Wishing for a brain valve that would choke off the pictures. Alcohol lullabies finally eased him.

The next morning, he drove to a newsstand and picked up the morning's *Times* and *Herald-Examiner*. No reporter had called him or Schwinn on the Ingalls murder, but something that ugly was sure to be covered.

But it wasn't, not a line of print.

That made no sense. Reporters were tuned in to the police band, covered the morgue, too.

He sped to the station, checked his own box and Schwinn's for journalistic queries. Found only a single phone slip with his name at the top. Officer Del Monte from The Bel Air Patrol, no message. He dialed the number, talked to a few flat, bored voices before finally reaching Del Monte.

"Oh, yeah. You're the one called about parties." The guy had a crisp, clipped voice, and Milo knew he was talking to an ex–military man. Middle-aged voice. Korea, not V.N.

"That's right. Thanks for calling back. What've you got?"

"Two on Friday, both times kids being jerks. The first was a sweet sixteen on Stradella, all-girls sleep-over that some punks tried to crash. Not local boys. Black kids and Mexicans. The girls' parents called us, and we ejected them."

"Where were the crashers from?"

"They claimed Beverly Hills." Del Monte laughed. "Right."

"They give you any trouble?"

"Not up front. They made like they were leaving Bel Air—we followed them to Sunset, then hung back and watched. Idiots crossed over near UCLA, then tried to come back a few minutes later and head over to the other party." Del Monte chuckled, again. "No luck, Pachuco. Our people were already there on a neighbor complaint. We ejected them before they even got out of the car."

"Where was the second party?"

"That was the live one, big-time noise. Upper Stone Canyon Drive way above the hotel."

The locale Schwinn's source had mentioned. "Whose house?"

"Empty house," said Del Monte. "The family bought a bigger one but didn't get around to selling the first one and the parents took a vacation, left the kiddies behind and, big surprise, the kiddies decided to use the empty house for fun 'n' games, invited the entire damn city. Must've been two, three hundred kids all over the place, cars—Porsches and other good wheels, and plenty of outside wheels. By the time we showed up, it was a scene. It's a big property, coupla acres, no real close-by neighbors, but by now the closest neighbors were fed up."

"By now?" said Milo. "This wasn't the first time?"

Silence. "We've had a few other calls there. Tried to contact the parents, no luck, they're always out of town."

"Spoiled brats."

Del Monte laughed. "You didn't hear that from me. Anyway, what's up with all this?"

"Tracing a 187 victim's whereabouts."

Silence. "Homicide? Nah, no way. This was just kids partying and playing music too loud."

"I'm sure you're right," said Milo. "But I've got rumors that my db might've attended a party on the Westside, so I've gotta ask. What's the name of the family that owns the house?"

Longer silence. "Listen," said Del Monte. "These people—you do me wrong, I could be parking cars. And believe me, no one saw anything worse than drinking and screwing around—a few joints, big deal, right? Anyway, we closed it down."

"I'm just going through the routine, Officer," said Milo. "Your name won't come up. But if I don't check it out, *I'll* be parking cars. Who owns the house and what's the address?"

"A rumor?" said Del Monte. "There had to be tons of parties Friday night."

"Any party we hear about, we look into. That's why yours won't stick out."

"Okay . . . the family's named Cossack." Del Monte uttered it weightily, as if that was supposed to mean something.

"Cossack," said Milo, keeping his tone ambiguous.

"As in office buildings, shopping malls—Garvey Cossack. Big downtown developer, part of that bunch wanted to bring another football team to L.A."

"Yeah, sure," lied Milo. His interest in sports had peaked with Pop Warner baseball. "Cossack on Stone Canyon. What's the address?"

Del Monte sighed and read off the numbers.

"How many kids in the family?" said Milo.

"Three—two boys and a girl. Didn't see the daughter, there, but she could've been."

"You know the kids personally?"

"Nah, just by sight."

"So the boys threw the party," said Milo. "Names?"

"The big one's Garvey, Jr. and the younger one's Bob but they call him Bobo."

"How old?"

"Junior's probably twenty-one, twenty-two, Bobo's maybe a year younger."

*More than kids,* thought Milo.

"They gave us no trouble," said Del Monte. "They're just a couple guys like to have fun."

"And the girl?"

"Her I didn't see."

Milo thought he picked up something new in Del Monte's voice. "Name?"

"Caroline."

"Age?"

"Younger—maybe seventeen. It was really no big deal, everyone dispersed. My message said you're Central. Where was your db found?"

Milo told him.

"There you go," said Del Monte. "Fifteen miles from Bel Air. You're wasting your time."

"Probably. Three hundred partying kids just caved when you showed up?"

"We've got experience with that kind of thing."

"What's the technique?" said Milo.

"Use sensitivity," said the rent-a-cop. "Don't treat 'em like you would a punk from Watts or East L.A. 'cause these kids are accustomed to a certain style."

"Which is?"

"Being treated like they're important. If that doesn't work, threaten to call the parents."

"And if that doesn't work?"

"That usually works. Gotta go, nice talking to you."

"I appreciate the time, Officer. Listen, if I came by and showed a photo around, would there be a chance anyone would recognize a face?"

"Whose face?"

"The vic's."

"No way. Like I said, it was a swarm. After a while they all start to look alike."

"Rich kids?"

"Any kids."

It was nearly 10 A.M., and Schwinn still hadn't shown up. Figuring sooner rather than later was the best time to spring Janie's photo on Del Monte and his patrol buddies, Milo threw on his jacket and left the station.

Del Monte had been decent enough to call and look where it got him.

No good deed goes unpunished.

\* \* \*

It took nearly forty minutes to reach Bel Air. The patrol office was a white, tile-roofed bungalow tucked behind the west gate. Lots of architectural detail inside and out—Milo would've been happy to make it his house. He'd heard that the gates and the private-cop scrutiny had been instituted by Howard Hughes when he lived in Bel Air because the billionaire didn't trust LAPD.

The rich taking care of their own. Just like the party on Stone Canyon: ticked-off neighbors, but everything kept private, no nuisance call had reached the West L.A. station.

Del Monte was at the front desk, and when Milo came in, his dark, round face turned sour. Milo apologized and whipped out a crime-scene snap he'd taken from the pile Schwinn had left in his desk. The least horrifying of the collection—side view of Janie's face, just the hint of ligature ring around the neck. Del Monte's response was a cursory head flick. Two other guards were drinking coffee, and they gave the picture more careful study, then shook their heads. Milo would have liked to show Melinda Waters's photo, but Schwinn had pocketed it.

He left the patrol office and drove to the party house on Stone Canyon Drive. Huge, redbrick, three-story, six-column colonial. Black double doors, black shutters, mullioned windows, multiple gables. Milo's guess was twenty, twenty-five rooms.

The Cossack family had moved to something more generous.

A huge dry lawn and flaking paint on some of the shutters said the maintenance schedule had slackened since the house had emptied. Shredded hedges and scraps of paper confettiing the brick walkway were the only evidence of revelry gone too far. Milo parked, got out, picked up one of the shreds, hoping for some writing, but it was soft and absorbent and blank—heavy-duty paper towel. The gate to the backyard was bolted and opaque. He peered over, saw a big blue egg of a pool, rolling greenery, lots of brick patio, blue jays pecking. Behind one of the hedges, the glint of glass—cans and bottles.

The nearest neighbor was to the south, well separated from the colonial by the broad lawns of both houses. A much smaller, meticulously maintained one-story ranch emblazoned with flower beds and fronted by dwarf junipers trimmed Japanese-style. The northern border of the Cossack property was marked by a ten-foot stone wall that went on for a good thousand feet up Stone Canyon. Probably some multiacre estate, a humongous château pushed back too far from the street to be visible.

Milo walked across the dry lawn and the colonial's empty driveway, up to the ranch house's front door. Teak door, with a shiny brass knocker shaped like a swan. Off to the right a small cement Shinto shrine presided over a tiny, babbling stream.

A very tall woman in her late sixties answered his ring. Stout and regal with puffy, rouged cheeks, she wore her silver hair tied back in a bun so tight it looked painful, had sheathed her impressive frame in a cream kimono hand-painted with herons and butterflies. In one liver-spotted hand was an ivory-handled brush with pointed bristles tipped with black ink. Even in black satin flat slippers she was nearly eye level with Milo. Heels would have made her a giantess.

"Ye-es?" Watchful eyes, deliberate contralto.

Out came the badge. "Detective Sturgis, Mrs. . . . ."

"Schwartzman. What brings a detective to Bel Air?"

"Well, ma'am, last Friday your neighbors had a party—"

"A party," she said, as if the description was absurd. She aimed the brush at the empty Colonial. "More like rooting at the trough. The aptly named Cossacks."

"Aptly named?"

"Barbarians," said Mrs. Schwartzman. "A scourge."

"You've had problems with them before."

"They lived there for less than two years, let the place go to seed. That's their pattern, apparently. Move in, degrade, move out."

"To something bigger."

"But of *course*. Bigger is better, right? They're vulgarians. No surprise, given what the father does."

"What does he do?"

"He destroys period architecture and substitutes grotesquerie. Packing cartons pretending to be office buildings, those drive-in monstrosities—strip malls. And *she* . . . desperately blond, the sweaty anxiety of an *arriviste*. Both of them gone all the time. No supervision for those brats."

"Mrs. Schwart—"

"If you'd care to be precise, it's Dr. Schwartzman."

"Pardon me, Doctor—"

"I'm an endocrinologist—retired. My husband is

Professor Arnold Schwartzman, the orthopedic surgeon. We've lived here twenty-eight years, had wonderful neighbors for twenty-six—the Cantwells, he was in metals, she was the loveliest person. The two of them passed on within months of each other. The house went into probate, and *they* bought it."

"Who lives on the other side?" said Milo, indicating the stone walls.

"Officially, Gerhard Loetz."

Milo shot her a puzzled look.

"German industrialist." As if everyone should know. "Baron Loetz has homes all over the world. Palaces, I've been told. He's rarely here. Which is fine with me, keeps the neighborhood quiet. Baron Loetz's property extends to the mountains, the deer come down to graze. We get all sorts of wildlife in the canyon. We love it. Everything was perfect until *they* moved in. Why are you asking all these questions?"

"A girl went missing," said Milo. "There's a rumor she attended a party on the Westside Friday night."

Dr. Schwartzman shook her head. "Well, I wouldn't know about that. Didn't get a close look at those hoodlums, didn't want to. Never left the house. Afraid to, if you'd like to know. I was alone, Professor Schwartzman was in Chicago, lecturing. Usually, that doesn't bother me, we have an alarm, used to have an Akita." The hand around the brush tightened. Man-sized knuckles bulged. "But Friday night was alarming. So *many* of them, running in and out, screaming like banshees. As usual, I called the patrol, had them stay until the last barbarian left. Even so, I was nervous. What if they came back?"

"But they didn't."

"No."

"So you never got close enough to see any of the kids."

"That's correct."

Milo considered showing her the death photo anyway. Decided against it. Maybe the story hadn't hit the papers because someone upstairs wanted it that way. Dr. Schwartzman's hostility to the Cossacks might very well fuel another rumor. Working alone like this, he didn't want to screw up big-time.

"The patrol," he said, "not the police—"

"That's what we do in Bel Air, Detective. We pay the patrol, so they respond. Your department, on the other hand—there seems to be a belief among law enforcement types that the problems of the . . . fortunate are trivial. I learned that the hard way, when Sumi—my doggie—was murdered."

"When was this?"

"Last summer. Someone poisoned him. I found him right there." Indicating the front lawn. "They unlatched the gate and fed him meat laced with rat poison. That time, I did call your department, and they finally sent someone out. A detective. Allegedly."

"Do you remember his name?"

Dr. Schwartzman gave a violent headshake. "Why would I? He barely gave me the time of day, clearly didn't take me seriously. Didn't even bother to go over there, just referred it to Animal Control, and all *they* offered to do was dispose of Sumi's body, thank you very much for nothing."

"They?" said Milo.

Schwartzman's brush pointed at the party house.

"You suspect one of the Cossacks poisoned Sumi?"

"I don't suspect, I know," said Schwartzman. "But I can't prove it. The daughter. She's mad, quite definitely. Walks around talking to herself, a bizarre look in her eyes, all hunched over. Wears the same clothes for days on end. And she brings black boys home—clearly not right. Sumi despised her. Dogs have a nose for madness. Anytime that crazy girl walked by, poor Sumi would fly into a rage, throw himself against the gate, it was all I could do to calm him down. And let me tell you, Detective, the only time he responded that way was to stranger intrusion. Protective, Akitas are, that's the whole point of an Akita. But sweet and smart—he loved the Cantwells, even grew accustomed to the gardeners and the mailman. But never to that girl. He knew when someone was wrong. Simply despised her. I'm sure she poisoned him. The day I found his poor body, I spied her. Watching me through a second-story window. That pair of mad eyes. Staring. I stared right back and waved my fist, and you'd better believe that drapery snapped back into place. *She* knew that *I* knew. But soon after, she came out and walked past me—right past me, staring. She's a frightening thing, that girl. Hopefully that party was the last time we'll see them around here."

"She was at the party?" said Milo.

Dr. Schwartzman crossed her arms across her bosom. "Have you been listening to me, young man? I told you, I didn't get close enough to check."

"Sorry," said Milo. "How old is she?"

"Seventeen or eighteen."

"Younger than her brothers."

"*Those* two," said Schwartzman. "So *arrogant*."

"Ever have any problems with the brothers other than parties?"

"All the time. Their attitude."

"Attitude?"

"Entitled," said Schwartzman. "Smug. Just thinking about them makes me angry, and anger is bad for my health, so I'm going to resume my calligraphy. Good day."

Before Milo could utter another syllable, the door slammed shut and he was staring at teak. No sense pushing it; *Frau Doktor* Schwartzman could probably beat him in an arm wrestle. He returned to the car, sat there wondering if anything she'd said mattered.

The Cossack brothers had a bad attitude. Like every other rich kid in L.A.

The sister, on the other hand, sounded anything but typical—if Schwartzman could be believed. And if Schwartzman's suspicion about her dog was right, Sister Cossack's quirkiness was something to worry about.

Seventeen years old made Caroline Cossack an age peer of Janie Ingalls and Melinda Waters. A rich girl with a wild side and access to the right toys might very well have attracted two street kids.

Taking black boys home. Racism aside, that spelled rebel. Someone willing to push the envelope.

Dope, a couple of party girls venturing from Hollywood into uncharted territory . . . still, it came down to nothing more than rumor, and he had nowhere to take it.

He stared at the empty party house, took in Bel Air silence, shabby grace, a lifestyle he'd never attain.

Feeling out of his element, every inch the ignorant rookie.

And now he had to report back to Schwinn.

*This is a whodunit. This likes to munch on your insides, then shit you out in pellets . . .*

The bastard's reproachful voice had crept into his head and camped there, obnoxious but authoritative.

While Milo'd spun his wheels, Schwinn had come up with the single useful lead on the Ingalls case: the tip that had led them straight to Janie's father.

A source he wouldn't identify. Not even bothering to be coy, coming right out and accusing Milo of spying for the brass.

Because he knew he was under suspicion? Maybe *that's* why the other D's seemed to shun the guy. Whatever was going on, Milo'd been shoved square in the middle of it . . . he had to push all that aside and concentrate on the *job*. But the job—going nowhere—made him feel inadequate.

Poor Janie. And Melinda Waters—what was the chance *she* was alive? What would *she* look like when they finally found her?

It was nearly noon and he couldn't remember the last time he'd eaten. But he could find no reason to stop for grease. Had no appetite for anything.

**CHAPTER**

# 10

**H**e arrived back at the station wondering if Schwinn had returned and hoping he hadn't. Before he made it to the stairwell, the desk sergeant said, "Someone's waiting for you," without looking up.

"Who?"

"Go see for yourself. Interview Five."

Something in the guy's voice pinged Milo's gut. "Interview Five?"

"Uh-huh." The blue kept his head down, busy with paperwork.

An interrogation room. Someone being questioned—a suspect for Ingalls in custody so soon? Had Schwinn pulled off another solo end run?

"I wouldn't keep them waiting," said the sergeant, writing something down, still avoiding eye contact.

Milo peered over the counter, saw a crossword puzzle book. "Them."

No answer.

Milo hurried down the too-bright corridor that housed the interview rooms and knocked on Five. A voice, not Schwinn's, said, "Come in."

He opened the door and came face-to-face with two tall men in their thirties. Both were broad-shouldered and good-looking, in well-cut charcoal suits, starched white shirts, and blue silk ties.

Corporate Bobbsey twins—except one guy was white—Swedish pink, actually, with a crew cut the color of cornflakes—and the other was black as the night.

Together they nearly spanned the width of the tiny, stale room, a two-man offensive line. Black had opened the door. He had a smooth, round head topped by a razor-trimmed cap of ebony fuzz and glowing, hairless, blue-tinged skin. The clear, hard eyes of a drill instructor. His unsmiling mouth was a fissure in a tar pit.

Pinkie hung toward the rear of the tiny room, but he was the first to speak.

"Detective Sturgis. Have a seat." Reedy voice, Northern inflection—Wisconsin or Minnesota. He pointed to the room's solitary chair, a folding metal affair on the near side of the interrogation table, facing the one-way mirror. The mirror, not even close to subterfuge, every suspect knew he was being observed, the only question was by whom? And now Milo was wondering the same thing.

"Detective," said the black man. Offering him the *suspect* chair.

On the table was a big, ugly Setchell-Carlson reel-to-reel tape recorder, the same gray as the twins' suits. Everything color-coordinated—like some psychology experiment and guess who was the guinea pig . . .

"What's going on?" he said, remaining in the doorway.

"Come in and we'll tell you," said Pinkie.

"How about a proper introduction?" said Milo. "As in who are you and what's this all about?" Surprising himself with his assertiveness.

The suits weren't surprised. Both looked pleased, as if Milo had confirmed their expectation.

"Please come in," said Black, putting some steel into "please." He came closer, stepped within inches of Milo's nose, and Milo caught a whiff of expensive aftershave, something with citrus in it. The guy was taller than Milo—six-four or -five—and Pinkie looked every bit as big. Size was one of the few advantages Milo figured God had given him; for the most part, he'd used it to avoid confrontation. But between these guys and the Wagnerian Dr. Schwartzman it had been a bad day for exploiting body type.

"Detective," said Black. His face was strangely inanimate—an African war mask. And those eyes. The guy had presence; he was used to being in charge. That was curious. Since the Watts riots, there'd been some race progress in the department, but for the most part it was lip service. Blacks and Mexicans were despised by the brass, shunted to dead-end patrol jobs in the highest-crime segments of Newton, Southwest, and Central, with scant chance for advancement. But this guy—his suit looked like mohair blend, the stitching on the lapels, hand-sewn—what kind of dues had he paid and who the hell was he?

He stepped aside and as Milo entered the room, nodded approvingly. "In terms of an introduction, I'm Detective Broussard and this is Detective Poulsenn."

"Internal Affairs," said Poulsenn.

Broussard smiled. "In terms of why we want you here, it would be better if you sat down."

Milo settled on the folding chair.

Poulsenn remained in the far corner of the interrogation room, but cramped quarters placed him close enough for Milo to count the pores in his nose. If he'd had any. Like Broussard, his complexion glowed like a poster for clean living. Broussard positioned himself to Milo's right, angled so Milo had to crane to see his lips move.

"How do you like Central Division, Detective?"

"I like it fine." Milo chose not to strain to meet Broussard's eyes, kept his attention on Poulsenn but stayed inert and silent.

"Enjoying homicide work?" said Broussard.

"Yes, sir."

"What about homicide work do you like, specifically?"

"Solving problems," said Milo. "Righting wrongs."

"Righting wrongs," said Broussard, as if impressed by the originality of the response. "So homicide can be righted."

"Not in the strict sense." This was starting to feel like one of those stupid grad school seminars. Professor Milrad taking out his frustration on hapless students.

Poulsenn checked his fingernails. Broussard said, "Are you saying you enjoy trying to achieve justice?"

"Exactly—"

"Justice," said Poulsenn, "is the point of all police work."

"Yes, it is," said Broussard. "Sometimes, though, justice gets lost in the shuffle."

Slipping a question mark into the last few words. Milo didn't bite, and Broussard went on: "A shame when that happens, isn't it, Detective Sturgis?"

Poulsenn inched closer. Both IA men stared down at Milo.

He said, "I'm not getting the point of—"

"You were in Vietnam," said Broussard.

"Yes—"

"You were a medic, saw lots of action."

"Yes."

"And before that you earned a master's degree."

"Yes."

"Indiana University. American literature."

"Correct. Is there some—"

"Your partner, Detective Schwinn, never went to college," said Broussard. "In fact, he never finished high school, got grandfathered in back when that was acceptable. Did you know that?"

"No—"

"Nor did Detective Schwinn serve in any branch of the military. Too young for Korea, too old for 'Nam. Have you found that a problem?"

"A problem?"

"In terms of commonality. Developing rapport with Detective Schwinn."

"No, I . . ." Milo shut his mouth.

"You . . . ?" said Broussard.

"Nothing."

"You were about to say something, Detective."

"Not really."

"Oh, yes you were," said Broussard, suddenly

cheerful. Milo craned, involuntarily. Saw his purplish, bowed lips hooked up at the corners. But
Broussard's mouth locked shut, no teeth. "You were
definitely going to say something, Detective."

"I . . ."

"Let's recap, Detective, to refresh your memory. I
asked you if Detective Schwinn's lack of higher education and military service had posed a problem for
you in terms of rapport and you said, 'No, I . . .'. It
was fairly obvious that you changed your mind about
saying what you were going to say."

"There's no problem between Detective Schwinn
and myself. That's all I was going to say. We get along
fine."

"Do you?" said Poulsenn.

"Yes."

Broussard said, "So Detective Schwinn agrees with
your point of view."

"About what?"

"About justice."

"I—you'd have to ask him."

"You've never discussed weighty issues with Detective Schwinn?"

"No, as a matter of fact, we concentrate on our
cases—"

"You're telling us that Detective Schwinn has never
verbalized any feelings about the job to you? About
righting wrongs? Achieving justice? His attitude
toward police work?"

"Well," said Milo, "I can't really pinpoint—"

Poulsenn stepped forward and pushed the RECORD
button on the Setchell-Carlson. Kept going and ended

up inches from Milo's left side. Now both IA men were flanking him. Boxing him in.

Broussard said, "Are you aware of any improper behavior on the part of Detective Schwinn?"

"No—"

"Consider your words before you speak, Detective Sturgis. This is an official department inquiry."

"Into Detective Schwinn's behavior or mine?"

"Is there a reason to look into *your* behavior, Detective Sturgis?"

"No, but I didn't know there was any reason to look into Detective Schwinn's behavior."

"You didn't?" said Poulsenn. To Broussard: "His position seems to be that he's unaware."

Broussard clicked his tongue. Switched off the recorder, pulled something out of a jacket pocket. A sheaf of papers that he waved. Milo was craning hard now, saw the front sheet, the familiar layout of a photocopied mug shot.

Female arrestee, dead-eyed and dark-skinned. Mexican or a light-skinned black. Numbers hanging on her chest.

Broussard peeled off the sheet, held it in front of Milo's eyes.

*Darla Washington, DOB 5-14-54, HT. 5-06 WT. 134.*

Instinctively, Milo's eyes dropped to the penal code violation: P.C. 653.2.

*Loitering for the purpose of prostitution . . .*

"Have you ever met this woman?" said Broussard.

"Never."

"Not in the company of Detective Schwinn or anyone else?"

"Never."

"It wouldn't be in the company of anyone else," said Poulsenn, cheerfully.

Nothing happened for a full minute. The IA men letting that last bit of dialogue sink in. Letting Milo know that they knew he was the least likely man in the room to engage a female hooker?

Or was *he* being paranoid? This was about Schwinn, not him. *Right?*

He said, "Never saw her anywhere."

Broussard placed Darla Washington's sheet at the bottom of the stack, flashed the next page.

*LaTawna Hodgkins.*

P.C. 653.2.

"What about this woman?"

"Never saw her."

This time, Broussard didn't push, just moved to the next page. The game went on for a while, a collection of bored/stoned/sad-eyed streetwalkers, all black. Donna Lee Bumpers, Royanne Chambers, Quitha Martha Masterson, DeShawna Devine Smith.

Broussard shuffled the 653.2 deck like a Vegas pro. Poulsenn smiled and watched. Milo kept outwardly cool but his bowels were churning. Knowing exactly where this was going.

She was the eighth card dealt.

Different hair than last night's red extravagance—a bleached blond mushroom cloud that made her look ridiculous. But the face was the same.

Schwinn's backseat tumble.

*Tonya Marie Stumpf.* The Teutonic surname seemed incongruous, where had *that* come from—

The mug shot danced in front of him for a long

time, and he realized he hadn't responded to Broussard's, "And this woman?"

Broussard said, "Detective Sturgis?"

Milo's throat tightened and his face burned and he had trouble breathing. Like one of those anaphylactic reactions he'd seen as a medic. Perfectly healthy guys surviving firefights only to keel over from eating peanuts.

He felt as if *he'd* been force-fed something toxic. . .

"Detective Sturgis," Broussard repeated, nothing friendly in his tone.

"Yes, sir?"

"This woman. Have you seen her before?"

They'd been watching the unmarked, surveilling Schwinn and *him*—for how long? Had they been spying the Beaudry murder site? Snooped during the entire time he and Schwinn had been riding together?

So Schwinn's paranoia *had* been well justified. And yet, he'd picked up Tonya Stumpf and had her do him in the backseat, the stupid, no-impulse-control, sonofa—

"Detective Sturgis," Broussard demanded. "We need an answer."

A whir from the table distracted Milo. Tape reels, revolving slowly. When had the machine been switched on, again?

Milo broke out in a full-body sweat. Recalling Schwinn's tirade in front of Bowie Ingalls's building, the sudden, vicious distrust, convinced Milo was a plant, and now. . . .

*Told you so.*

"Detective," said Broussard. "Answer the question. *Now.*"

"Yes," said Milo.

"Yes, what?"

"I've seen her."

"Yes, you have, son," said Broussard, crouching low, exuding citrus and success.

*Son.* The asshole was only a few years older than Milo, but it was clear who had the power.

"You definitely *have* seen her."

They kept him in there for another hour and a half, taping his statement then replaying it, over and over. Explaining that they wanted to make sure everything had copied accurately, but Milo knew the real reason: wanting him to hear the fear and evasiveness in his own voice in order to instill self-loathing, soften him up for whatever they had in store.

He copped only to the basic details of Tonya's pickup—stuff they knew already—and resisted the pressure to elaborate. The room grew hot and rancid with fear as they changed the subject from Tonya to Schwinn's comportment, in general. Picking at him like gnats, wanting to hear about Schwinn's political views, racial attitudes, his opinions about law enforcement. Prodding, pushing, cajoling, threatening Milo subtly and not-so-subtly, until he felt as alive as chuck steak.

They returned to probing sexual details. He maintained his denial of witnessing any actual sexual encounters between Schwinn and Tonya or anyone else. Which was technically correct, he'd kept his eyes on the road, had harbored no desire to rearview peep the blow job.

When they asked about the conversation between

Schwinn and Tonya, he gave them some bullshit story about not hearing because it had all been whispers.

"Whispers," said Broussard. "You didn't think that was unusual? Detective Schwinn whispering to a known prostitute in the backseat of your department-issue vehicle?"

"I figured it for work talk. She was an informant, and Schwinn was pressing her for info."

Waiting for the obvious next question: "Info on what?" But it never came.

No questions at all about Janie Ingalls's murder or any other case he and Schwinn had worked.

"You thought she was an informant," said Poulsenn.

"That's what Detective Schwinn said."

"Then why the whispering?" said Broussard. "You're Detective Schwinn's alleged partner. Why would he keep secrets from you?"

*Because he knew this would happen, asshole.* Milo shrugged. "Maybe there was nothing to tell."

"Nothing to tell?"

"Not every snitch has something to offer," said Milo.

Broussard waved that off. "How long were Schwinn and Tonya Stumpf in the backseat of the car as *you* drove?"

"Not long—maybe a few minutes."

"Quantify that."

Knowing the car had probably been observed, Milo kept it close to the truth. "Ten, maybe fifteen minutes."

"After which Tonya Stumpf was dropped off."

"Correct."

"Where?"

"Eighth Street near Witmer."

"After she left the unmarked, where did she go?"

He named the Ranch Depot Steak House, but didn't mention Schwinn's funding of Tonya's dinner.

"Did money exchange hands?" said Poulsenn.

Not knowing how much they'd seen, he chanced a lie. "No."

Long silence.

"During the entire time," Broussard finally said, "you were driving."

"Correct."

"When Detective Schwinn asked you to stop to pick up Tonya Stumpf, you weren't at all concerned about being an accessory to prostitution?"

"I never saw any evidence of prosti—"

Broussard's hand slashed air. "Did Tonya Stumpf's mouth make contact with Detective Schwinn's penis?"

"Not that I—"

"If you were driving, never looked back, as you claim, how can you be so sure?"

"You asked me if I saw something. I didn't."

"I asked you if oral-genital contact occurred."

"Not that I saw."

"So Tonya Stumpf's mouth might have made contact with Detective Schwinn's penis without your seeing it?"

"All I can say is what I saw."

"Did Detective Schwinn's penis make contact with Tonya Stumpf's vagina or Tonya Stumpf's *anus*?"

"I never saw that." Was the bastard emphasizing *anus* because . . . ?

"Did Tonya Stumpf engage in physical intimacy of any sort with Detective Schwinn?"

"I never saw that," Milo repeated, wondering if they'd used some sort of night scope, had everything on film and he was burnt toast—

"Mouth on penis," said Poulsenn. "Yes or no?"

"No."

"Penis on or in vagina."

"No."

"Penis on or in *anus*."

Same emphasis. Definitely not coincidence. "No," said Milo, "and I think I'd better talk to a Protective League representative."

"Do you?" said Broussard.

"Yes, this is obviously—"

"You could do that, Detective Sturgis. If you think you really need representation. But why would you think that?"

Milo didn't answer.

"Do you have something to worry about, Detective?" said Broussard.

"I didn't until you guys hauled me in—"

"We didn't haul you, we invited you."

"Oh," said Milo. "My mistake."

Broussard touched the tape recorder, as if threatening to switch it on again. Leaned in so close Milo could count the stitches on his lapel. No pores. Not a single damn pore, the bastard was carved of ebony. "Detective Sturgis, you're not implying coercion, are you?"

"No—"

"Tell us about your relationship with Detective Schwinn."

Milo said, "We're partners, not buddies. Our time together is spent on work. We've cleared seven homicides in three months—one hundred percent of our calls. Recently, we picked up an eighth one, a serious whodunit that's gonna require—"

"Detective," said Broussard. Louder. Cutting off that avenue of conversation. "Have you ever witnessed Detective Schwinn receiving money from anyone during work hours?"

No desire to talk about Janie Ingalls.

Caught up in his headhunter ritual, one that wouldn't, couldn't be stopped, until it played itself out. Or something else: an *active* disinterest in Janie Ingalls?

Milo said, "No."

"Not with Tonya Stumpf?"

"No."

"Or anyone else?" barked Broussard.

"No," said Milo. "Never, not once."

Broussard lowered his face and stared into Milo's eyes. Milo felt his breath, warm, steady, minty—now suddenly sour, as if bile had surged up his gullet. So the guy had body processes after all.

"Not once," he repeated.

They let him go as abruptly as they'd hauled him in, no parting words, both IA men turning their backs on him. He left the station directly, didn't go upstairs to his desk or bother to check his messages.

The next morning a departmental notice appeared in his home mailbox. Plain white envelope, no postmark, hand-delivered.

Immediate transfer to the West L.A. station, some

gobbledygook about manpower allocation. A typed addendum said he'd already been assigned a locker there and listed the number. The contents of his desk and his personal effects had been moved from Central.

His outstanding cases had been transferred to other detectives.

He phoned Central, tried to find out who'd caught Janie Ingalls's murder, got a lot of runaround, finally learned that the case had left the station and gone to Metro Homicide—Parker Center's high-profile boys.

Kicked upstairs.

Metro loved publicity, and Milo figured finally Janie would hit the news.

But she didn't.

He phoned Metro, left half a dozen messages, wanting to give them the information he hadn't had time to chart in the Ingalls murder book. The Cossack party, Melinda Waters's disappearance, Dr. Schwartzman's suspicions about Caroline Cossack.

No one returned his calls.

At West L.A., his new lieutenant was piggish and hostile, and Milo's assignment to a partner was delayed—more department gibberish. A huge pile of stale 187s and a few new ones—idiot cases, luckily—landed on his desk. He rode alone, walked through the job like a robot, disoriented by his new surroundings. West L.A. had the lowest crime stats in the city, and he found himself missing the rhythm of the bloody streets.

He made no effort to make friends, avoided socializing after hours. Not that invitations came his way. The Westside's D's were even colder than his Central colleagues, and he wondered how much of it could be blamed on his pairing with Schwinn, maybe picking up a snitch jacket. Or had the rumors followed him here, too?

Fag cop. Fag *snitch* cop? A few weeks in, a cop named Wes Baker tried to be social—telling Milo he'd heard Milo had a master's, it was about time someone with brains went into police work. Baker figured himself for an intellectual, played chess, lived in an apartment full of books and used big words when small ones would've sufficed. Milo saw him as a pretentious jerk, but allowed Baker to rope him in on double dates with his girlfriend and her stewardess pals. Then one night Baker drove by and spotted him standing on a West Hollywood street corner, waiting for the light to change. The only men out walking were seeking other men, and Baker's silent stare told Milo plenty.

Shortly after, someone broke into Milo's locker and left a stash of sadomasochistic gay porn.

A week after that, Delano Hardy—the station's only black D—was assigned to be his partner. The first few weeks of their rides were tight-lipped, worse than with Schwinn, almost unbearably tense. Del was a religious Baptist who'd run afoul of the brass by criticizing the department's racial policies, but he had no use for sexual nonconformity. News of the porn stash had gotten round; ice-eyes seemed to follow Milo around.

Then things eased. Del turned out to be psychologically flexible—a meticulous, straight arrow with good instincts and an obsession with doing the job. The two of them began working as a team, solved case after case, forged a bond based on success and the avoidance of certain topics. Within six months, they were in the groove, putting away bad guys with no sweat. *Neither* of them invited to station house barbecues, bar crawls. Cop-groupie gang bangs.

When the workday was over, Del returned to a Leimert Park tract home and his upright, uptight wife who still didn't know about Milo, and Milo skulked back to his lonely-guy pad. But for the Ingalls case, he had a near-perfect solve rate.

But for the Ingalls case . . .

He never saw Pierce Schwinn again, heard a rumor the guy had taken early retirement. A few months later he called Parker Center Personnel, lied, managed to learn that Schwinn had left with no record of disciplinary action.

So maybe it had nothing to do with Schwinn, after all, and everything to do with Janie Ingalls. Emboldened, he phoned Metro again, fishing for news on the case. Again, no callback. He tried Records, just in case someone had closed it, was informed they had no listing of the case as solved, no sighting of Melinda Waters.

One hot July morning, he woke up dreaming about Janie's corpse, drove over to Hollywood, and cruised by Bowie Ingalls's flop on Edgemont. The pink building was gone, razed to the dirt, the soil chewed out for a subterranean parking lot, the beginnings of framework set in place. The skeleton of a much larger apartment building.

He drove to Gower and headed a mile north. Eileen Waters's shabby little house was still standing but Waters was gone and two slender, effeminate young men—antiques dealers—were living there. Within moments, both were flirting outrageously with Milo, and that scared him. He'd put on all the cop macho, and still they could tell . . .

The pretty-boys were renting, the house had been vacant when they'd moved in, neither had any idea where the previous tenant had gone.

"I'll tell you one thing," said one of the lads. "She was a smoker. The place reeked."

"Disgusting," agreed his roomie. "We cleaned up everything, went neo-Biedermeier. You wouldn't recognize it." Grinning conspiratorially. "So tell us. What did she *do*?"

# 11

**M**ilo finished the story and walked into my kitchen.

The beeline to the fridge, finally.

I watched him open the freezer compartment where the bottle of Stolichnaya sat. The vodka had been a gift from him to Robin and me, though I rarely touched anything other than Scotch or beer and Robin drank wine.

Robin . . .

I watched him fill half a glass, splash in some grapefruit juice for color. He drained the glass, poured a refill, returned to the dining room table.

"That's it," he said.

I said, "A black detective named Broussard. As in . . ."

"Yup."

"Ah."

Tossing back the second vodka, he returned to the kitchen, fixed a third glass, more booze, no juice. I thought of saying something—sometimes he wants me to play that role. Remembered how much Chivas

I'd downed since Robin's departure and held my tongue.

This time when he returned, he sat down heavily, wrapped thick hands around the glass, and swirled, creating a tiny vodka whirlpool.

"John G. Broussard," I said.

"None other."

"The way he and the other guy leaned on you. Sounds Kafkaesque."

He smiled. "Today I woke up as a cockroach? Yeah, good old John G. had a knack for that kind of thing from way back. Served the lad well, hasn't it?"

John Gerald Broussard had been L.A.'s chief of police for a little over two years. Handpicked by the outgoing mayor, in what many claimed was an obvious pander aimed at neutralizing critics of LAPD's racial problems, Broussard had a military bearing and a staggeringly imperious personality. The City Council distrusted him, and most of his own officers—even black cops—despised him because of his headhunter background. Broussard's open disdain for anyone who questioned his decisions, his apparent disinterest in the details of street policing, and his obsession with interdepartmental discipline helped complete the picture. Broussard seemed to revel in his lack of popularity. At his swearing-in ceremony, decked out as usual in full dress uniform and a chestful of ribbon candy, the new chief laid out his number one priority: zero tolerance for any infractions by police officers. The following day, Broussard dissolved a beloved system of community-police liaison outposts in high-crime neighborhoods, claiming they did nothing to reduce felonies and that excessive fraternization with citizens "deprofessionalized" the department.

"Spotless John Broussard," I said. "And maybe he helped bury the Ingalls case. Any idea why?"

He didn't answer, drank some more, glanced again at the murder book.

"Looks like it was really sent to you," I said.

Still no reply. I let a few more moments pass. "Did anything ever develop on Ingalls?"

He shook his head.

"Melinda Waters never showed up?"

"I wouldn't know if she did," he said. "Once I got to West L.A., I didn't pursue it. For all I know, she got married, had kids, is living in a nice little house with a big-screen TV."

Talking too fast, too loud. I knew confession when I heard it.

He ran a finger under his collar. His forehead was shiny, and the stress cracks around his mouth and eyes had deepened.

He finished the third vodka, stood, and aimed his bulk back at the kitchen.

"Thirsty," I said.

He froze, wheeled. Glared. "Look who's talking. Your eyes. You gonna tell me you've been dry?"

"This morning I have been," I said.

"Congratulations. Where's Robin?" he demanded. "What the hell's going on with you two?"

"Well," I said, "my mail's been interesting."

"Yeah, yeah. Where is she, Alex?"

Words filled my head but logjammed somewhere in my throat. My breath got short. We stared at each other.

He laughed first. "Show you mine if you show me yours?"

I told him the basics.

"So it was an opportunity for her," he said. "She'll get it out of her system, and come back."

"Maybe," I said.

"It happened before, Alex."

*Thanks for the memory, pal.* I said, "This time I can't help thinking it's more. She kept the offer from me for two weeks."

"You were busy," he said.

"I don't think that's it. The way she looked at me in Paris. The way she left. The fault line might have shifted too much."

"C'mon," he said, "how about some optimism? You're always preaching to me about that."

"I don't preach. I suggest."

"Then I *suggest* you shave and scrape the crud from your eyes and get into clean clothes, stop ignoring her calls, and try to work things out, for God's sake. You guys are like . . ."

"Like what?"

"I was gonna say an old married couple."

"But we're not," I said. "Married. All these years together and neither of us took the initiative to make it legal. What does that say?"

"You didn't need the paperwork. Believe me, I know all about that."

He and Rick had been together even longer than Robin and I.

"Would you if you could?" I said.

"Probably," he said. "Maybe. What's the big issue between you guys, anyway?"

"It's complicated," I said. "And I haven't been avoiding her. We just keep missing each other."

"Try harder."

"She's on the road, Milo."

"Try harder, anyway, goddammit."

"What's *with* you?" I said.

"Acute *disillusionment*. On top of all the chronic disillusionment the job deals me." He clapped a hand on my shoulder. "I need some things in my life to be constant, pal. As in you guys. I want Robin and you to be okay for *my* peace of mind, okay? Is that too much to ask? Yeah, yeah, it's self-centered, but tough shit."

What can you say to that?

I sat there, and he swiped at his brow. More sweat leaked through. He looked thoroughly miserable. Crazily enough, I felt guilty.

"We'll work it out," I heard myself saying. "Now tell me why you looked like death when you saw Janie Ingalls's photo?"

"Low blood sugar," he said. "No time for breakfast."

"Ah," I said. "Hence the vodka."

He shrugged. "I thought it was out of my head, but maybe I figure I should've pursued it."

"Maybe 'NS' means someone else thinks you should pursue it now. Do any of the other photos in the book mean anything to you?"

"Nope."

I looked at the gloves he'd discarded. "Going to run prints?"

"Maybe," he said. Then he grimaced.

"What?"

"Ghost of failures past."

He poured a fourth glass, mostly juice, maybe an ounce of vodka.

I said, "Any guesses who sent it?"

"Sounds like you've got one."

"Your ex-partner, Schwinn. He had a fondness for photography. And access to old police files."

"Why the hell would he be contacting me, now? He couldn't stand me. Didn't give a damn about the Ingalls case or any other."

"Maybe time has mellowed him. He worked Homicide for twenty years before you came on. Meaning he'd have been on the job during much of the period covered by the photos. The ones that preceded his watch, he swiped. He bent the rules, so lifting a few crime-scene photos wouldn't have been much of an ethical stretch. The book could be part of a collection he assembled over the years. He called it the murder book and bound it in blue, to be cute."

"But why send it to me *via* you? Why now? What's his damn point?"

"Is Janie's picture one Schwinn could've snapped himself?"

Peeling on a new pair of gloves, he flipped back to the death shot.

"Nah, this is professionally developed, better quality than what he'd have gotten with that Instamatic."

"Maybe he had the film reprocessed. Or if he's still a photography bug, he's got himself a home darkroom."